Hootcat
Hill

Hootcat Hill

Lucy Coats

Orion
Children's Books

First published in Great Britain in 2008
by Orion Children's Books
a division of the Orion Publishing Group Ltd
Orion House
5 Upper St Martin's Lane
London WC2H 9EA
An Hachette Livre UK company

1 3 5 7 9 10 8 6 4 2

A catalogue record for this book is
available from the British Library.

ISBN 978 1 84255 614 6

Printed in Great Britain
Clays Ltd, St Ives plc

The Orion Publishing Group's policy is to use papers
that are natural, renewable and recyclable products made
from wood grown in sustainable forests. The logging and
manufacturing processes are expected to conform to the
environmental regulations of the country of origin.

www.orionbooks.co.uk

*This is again for my husband, Richard,
who read, encouraged, upheld my spirits and
generally stuck in there for the long haul,
as he always does.*

With all my love, L.C.

Contents

One	A Maiden is Born	1
Two	The Greed of Young Tom Bickerspike	8
Three	Linnet Perry	18
Four	Visions in the Water, Signs in the Air	25
Five	The Calling of the Maiden	43
Six	The Meeting on Hootcat Hill	62
Seven	Lessons in Power	76
Eight	The Misery of Magret	89
Nine	Missing Persons	111
Ten	The Door to Avvallon	127
Eleven	Woodcock and Rowanberry	137
Twelve	Maiden and Prince	150
Thirteen	The Chalice of Athyr	165
Fourteen	The Caves of Lirrannan	178
Fifteen	Two Rescues – and a Nasty Surprise	187
Sixteen	Wyrm's Rise	202
Seventeen	Wyrm's Fall	208
Eighteen	Endings	213

Hootcat Hill

chapter one

A Maiden is Born

'Behind her ear a triple mole
and hair of white doth show.
By these and eyes of blue and green
The Maiden ye shall know'

from 'The Prophecies of the Seven'

The young badger was curled in his bracken bed, dreaming of a dragon – a black wyrm with red eyes which wove its nightmare coils around and about the heart of the world – when the cry of a newborn baby girl woke him suddenly from sleep. Startled, he opened his eyes to see a bright silhouette blazing out from among seven runes carved deep into the rock wall at the back of his cave. He looked up at the shining three-leaved shape and listened intently for a minute or so as the baby's crying continued. Then another sound joined the crying – twining round it in a faraway owl chorus of screeching, hooting noise. The badger nodded his head, strangely marked with a golden sunburst in the centre of his muzzle.

'Hootcat Hill has spoken,' he said. 'She is here.'

Outside, in a cottage on the eastern edge of the town of Wyrmesbury, a mother stared deep into her newborn daughter's eyes as the earth shivered and shrugged beneath her feet.

'One blue eye, one green,' she said to her husband, rocking the baby to calm her.

'And a mole like a trefoil behind her right ear,' said the proud father. 'What shall we call her?'

'I had a dream two nights ago,' said Nyneve Perry, looking up at him. 'You know I don't have dreams – ever – unless it's really important. But two nights ago I saw a little girl riding on the back of a white horse made of clouds. Three birds were flying round her head singing, "Linnet, Linnet, Linnet." I can't get the name out of my mind.'

'Hmmn,' said Merrilin Perry doubtfully, listening to his daughter's furious cries. 'She sounds more like those hootcat owls squalling outside than a Linnet at the moment, but I am sure she will get better at it. And it's wise to follow your dreams, particularly in Wyrmesbury.' He took the baby from her mother's arms and regarded her gravely. She fell silent and stared back into her father's eyes.

'Welcome to this world, Linnet Perry,' he said.

Sunstar the Badger waddled over to the seven runes and ran his paws over them, tracing their shapes gently. 'First the Maiden's trefoil,' he muttered, as the blazing light faded from it, 'then my badger's claw.' Leaving these two alone, he briskly tapped the five remaining runes.

'Stagman, awake!' he said, rapping an antler shape.

'Daughter of Mares, awake!' rapping a horseshoe.

'Wyccan, awake!' rapping a cauldron.

'Smith, awake!' rapping an anvil.

'Owlman, awake!' rapping a flying hootcat owl. 'The Maiden is born into the world again, and the worldwyrm stirs in my dreams and in his bed.'

'Let her not be needed in our time of Guarding,' came the ritual reply from five voices inside his head.

'Let her not be needed,' he said gravely, before breaking the link. He sighed heavily and settled down on his bracken bed to remember the lore of the Guardians once more. Would the worldwyrm be woken in this Maiden's time? Would this baby girl be the first to be needed for nearly five hundred turnings of the seasons in the world outside?

'Claws crossed, I do hope not,' he muttered, as the hootcat screeches died away outside.

There were to be no more girl babies born in Wyrmesbury for seven years, only boys. The Maiden had come into the world alone as always.

Linnet Perry woke gasping from a nightmare to find her room full of morning. She shivered. What had she dreamed? Something about Young Tom Bickerspike being swallowed by a dragon. Or was it a great yellow technomachine? Surely she had nearly been shaken out of her bed by the shuddering as they sank deep into the earth? Warm sun-dapples chased across her face, even though the sun had not yet risen, touching her with friendly fingers that wiped away the darkness of the wyrm's belly and Young Tom's screaming, terrified face from her mind. But Linnet did not notice. She set her feet onto the bare boards beside her bed, and wriggled them into warm slippers. It was early. Much too early to be getting dressed for school, so she went over to the low window that faced the garden and knelt down to look out at the day.

The real sun was just climbing up over Hootcat Hill, making the dark trees that crowned it look even more mysterious than usual. The hootcats that gave the hill its name were silent this morning, but Linnet had heard them last night. In her dream. She shivered briefly, then squinted her eyes and tried to see the Owlstones through the thickets of trees, but they were wreathed in the heavy mist which always surrounded them, and she couldn't distinguish them at all. Then her eyes and her mind drifted away, as everyone's in Wyrmesbury always did if they looked at or thought about Hootcat Hill for too long.

The primroses and early honeysuckles were blossoming in the cottage garden below, and she opened the window and leaned out to take a long breath of their sweet scent. As she looked, a large badger waddled out of the hedge that divided the garden from the fields below the eastern edge of the town and sniffed the air suspiciously. He was a huge boar, with deep black flanks, and a brilliant white stripe down the middle of his head. He had a strange golden marking in the centre of his forehead, just above his eyes, which looked like a starry sunburst.

The badger had a sett in the old mound far down in the field on the other side of the hedge, and Linnet saw him so often that she sometimes thought he was keeping an eye on her. Perhaps seeing him today was a good omen, she thought. She was dreading her Frankish test, but she was dreading what They might do to her at school even more. Her best friend Petroc Suleymann would not be there today because he had had to go and visit his sick grandmother for a few days.

Linnet felt a surge of sudden anger at the thought of Them. Why did They have to make school life so difficult for her? She thumped an angry fist on the windowsill. She was so tired of being called the weirdo of Wyrmesbury and pinched and kicked by the Vesterton kids, just because she had a funny white streak in her hair, different coloured eyes, and lived in a place with a reputation for oddness, not to mention the difficulties she had with reading and spelling. And They didn't even know about the other stuff – the dream stuff and the secret stuff that made her really and truly weird. Only Petroc knew about that, and she didn't even tell him all of it.

She clenched her jaw, remembering last week when They'd caught her away from Petroc and stuffed her head down a toilet, but as usual she couldn't think of any way to change things. Whatever she tried – ignoring Them, trying to suck up to Them, hitting Them back, running away – none of it made any difference. She still came out of school either black and blue or with her books ripped and torn at least twice a week. Her friend Magret, Young Tom's sister, generally helped her to mend any really bad book tears on the bus journey home – and she always wore trousers and long sleeves to cover up the bruises so her parents wouldn't notice.

Linnet was too ashamed to tell her parents about any of it, though Magret and Petroc were forever nagging her to. Her Wyrmesbury-born father just might understand – he'd had to go to school in Vesterton himself and deal with his own problems – but her outsider-bred mother would either make a huge fuss with the school (which didn't bear thinking about), or, more likely, not listen properly as usual, because she was too busy. It just wasn't worth the hassle of explaining it all, anyway. She'd manage, like she always had, and school wouldn't be forever.

Then the badger snorted, recalling her to the present. Linnet smiled and waved at him.

'Good morning, badger,' she whispered, feeling better just at the sight of him. The badger looked up at her.

'Hail and good morrow, Linnet the Maiden,' he said gravely, just inside her head. 'Come and visit me in the mound tonight.' Linnet blinked and shook her head wildly to clear her ears. The secret stuff meant that she sometimes saw strange colours round other people, and flickering lights in the corner of her eye that she was too scared to look at properly because it might be magic – but she'd never had an animal speak to her before, let alone being asked to visit one.

'Did you really say that?' she asked him. But the badger only grunted contemptuously and waddled off back through the hedge. Linnet shrugged. 'Must have imagined it. Animals don't talk – even in Wyrmesbury.' But in her heart she knew it had been real. She felt scared again, the nightmare images of Young Tom's screams flooding back into her head. Suddenly, beside her bed the alarm clock began to shrill and shake, ruining the morning quietness, and she rushed to turn it off.

chapter two

The Greed of Young Tom Bickerspike

*'When strange winds rush
through valley's hush,
and earth is pierced for gold,
then will the worldwyrm claim its toll
and the Maiden's fate unfold . . .'*

from 'The Prophecies of the Seven'

Late in the stillness of the night before, Young Tom Bickerspike stood gloating at the edge of a huge drillhole. The moon was rising, and nearly full, and the mud rainbows shone in its white light. The earth moved gently under his feet – a small warning shudder of unease.

'Tomorrow,' he said aloud. 'Tomorrow we'll drill deep enough to see.' Young Tom's eyes glinted with greed and he licked his lips and went into a daydream at the thought of all the riches his oily black gold would bring him. Soon, at just seventeen, he would have more money than all his posh Oxenfoord friends put together. The start of the new University term was in just two days, and when he went back he would have all the funds he needed to buy the fast cars he so craved, and his little sister, Magret, would have all the pretty dresses their mean old father had never bought her. Even better, he wouldn't have to come home every holidays to work on his farm any more. Brains like his were not destined to plough fields and feed cows. He was a new breed of Bickerspike, he decided. He would be a rich master of the technoworld, not just a grubby farmer like his ancestors.

A small silent click, and then a soft creak sounded beside him.

'Tomorrow,' he whispered again. Then he looked up at the yellow technomachine. The shiny seat in the cab glinted invitingly and the door was ajar. Young Tom frowned, for he could have sworn the operator had locked it before he left, but then he shrugged his shoulders and climbed up and in. The keys were still in the ignition, and as he fingered them possessively, a mood of wild teenage recklessness came over him.

'Why not see right now?' he said loudly as the wild wind came rushing down the valley from the seven hills and rocked him and the technomachine warningly. The ground shuddered again, and the yellow technomachine sank a little into the thick mud, groaning to itself.

The Fey Queen smelt the stink of the young human male's greed at once. She bared her teeth and hissed. Oh! How she hated mortals. It was a mortal Maiden and her inquisitiveness who had trapped her and half her people in this dank, dark underworld. It was the fault of a mortal Maiden that she had been condemned to live apart from her Prince for ages past, seeing him only for a brief moment at the time of Changeover.

The Fey Queen sighed. It was almost time for the Prince to take her place, while she returned to the otherworld of Avvallon. She was so drained that she couldn't even summon the smallest speck of excitement at the idea.

It had been such a small mistake to make, she thought. Such a small piece of malicious Fey mischief to punish that long-ago human child for her curiosity, with such an unexpected result. The never-ending punishment for the wyrm's first waking meant that, apart from the guard duty laid upon her and her people, her Fey queenly beauty was changed in this place into a repulsive thing of transparent green – because she could only survive here in that vile form. There was no dancing except for the death dance or the warning dance, no music except that which destroyed, no jewels to adorn her, no hunting the White Stag in the sunlit glades of Avvallon, no magical Fey flower-rings to bring enchantment under the moonlight, no long days playing in the waves with the Merr King's children. And worst of all in this awful mortal world, no cunning Fidget Reedglitter to plot and spy for her, to take care of her, to make difficult decisions so that she could rule a court of pleasure and parties. If her insubstantial eyes had allowed her to weep, she would have.

The great black head moved restlessly under her, and

she began frantically to cast the old spells of sleep and guarding as the earth above shook slightly. The enchantments felt weak and feeble, and she knew that her Power was fading again as the Changeover approached. The wyrm was truly shifting in its bed now, rising upwards as it too smelt the greed, and felt something else too – something that screeched metallically as it battered and pierced the black, oily earth above its bed. The Fey Queen summoned her people to the surface urgently. The worldwyrm was surely being woken for the first time in five hundred years, and if the Fey could not make it sleep again it was time for another mortal to die.

'And serve him right,' snarled the Fey Queen viciously, as she and her people burst up out of the earth and began the dance of warning.

Tom turned the keys with a hasty flourish, pressing on the lever that said 'Drill', and the great screw sprang to life, turning, forcing its way down, down deep into the earth with a rasping scream. It was marvellous, powerful, and Tom felt like a god until the drill bucked and plunged under his hand as it hit something hard and unyielding. Then the scream was not only the drill's, for Tom was screaming now too. Shining, filmy, transparent green bodies rose up out of the ground around him, looking at him with haggard, inhuman eyes set in wild, untamed faces. One in particular came right up to him, her long green hair flying, her feet stamping and whirling until his head was spinning with terror.

Then the mud itself reared up in front of him in nightmare wyrm shape; it was opening into a fearsome mouth, it was lifting the technomachine – piercing the metal with its dagger claws, it was gulping the technomachine with Tom still inside it, struggling, struggling to get out and still screaming, down, down into the dark of a long, long black throat swallowing. The mud closed up and lay still. A pair of red eyes with slanted golden pupils glinted balefully at the moon and then slid down into silence. The shining shapes faded into a dense pearly mist which covered the ground with a malignant pale greenish sheen that stank of magic to those with the right sort of nose. The technomachine and Young Tom Bickerspike had disappeared from Black Meadows as if they had never been . . .

On Hootcat Hill, the Owlstones screeched noisily at the empty sky.

Those Three of the Six Guardians who were mostly human did not listen much to street gossip as a rule. They preferred to rely on their own prophecies and the signs and portents the winds had been blowing down from the hills since the end of winter. But the stories about Young Tom Bickerspike's strange disappearance had been running around the town like hot fear since just past seven o'clock.

As soon as Professor Tyto Hullart, curator and librarian of Wyrmesbury, heard the scared whispers in the newsagents on the corner of Gold Street and Leaf Street when he called in for his early morning paper, he hurried down to the farmers' marketplace. He needed some cheese, and it was the best place to pick up the latest street gossip and see if the whispers were truth. Coupled with that morning's earth tremor, the one of the previous night and the hootcats' warning from the stones, his growing unease was enough to make him pay close attention to the swiftly spreading rumours, because it was most unlike Wyrmesbury folk to be this frightened.

The market was already buzzing like a hive – and all the stalls were full, except for part of one in the far corner.

'Hello, Professor,' called Mrs Huggins from her cheese stall, seeing him staring at the empty space on her counter. 'It's no use you looking for eggs from Magret Bickerspike today. Poor girl's in too much of a state to collect them, what with all the police buzzing about the place. Young Tom's disappeared – taken a gurt big digger and run off! What do you think of that – a nice boy like him with his cleverness and going up to the university at Oxenfoord so young.'

'Who would have thought it?' said the Professor absently. 'Yes, I'll take a small slice of the Cheshire with herbs, Mrs Huggins, thank you.' As he listened with half an ear to Mrs Huggins telling her tale of disappeared technomachinery and mystery, he thought about the Bickerspikes, and Young Tom in particular. Bickerspikes had farmed the valley land by the river below Wyrmesbury for generations, making a tidy profit from grain and beast, adding a field here and there when they could buy it, building a fine house made with stone from the quarries above High Furling, and sturdy wooden barns that would weather the wild winds that sometimes swept down the Ash valley and over the farm for no reason, even on the clearest day.

Mrs Huggins handed him his cheese, still talking. 'Bickerspikes've always been careful folk, see, traditional, you might say. But Young Tom's half a Knapwort on his mother's side – that's where the brains come from in him and Magret. All sorts of plans he had for the land after his dad and the rest died last year so sudden. They say he was all for digging up Black Meadows.' She stopped suddenly. 'Black Meadows,' she said in a quiet, scared voice. 'Where them old fairies are said to live. Bad luck that is, to meddle with them. Or so my grandma always said.'

'Bad luck indeed,' said Professor Hullart, thanking Mrs Huggins and scratching his head thoughtfully as he strolled on past the chattering crowds. Stray conversations floated across on the breeze.

'What about that funny-coloured green mist what wouldn't clear? Strange that is, an' all,' said Tim Pritchett, weighing out bacon for Jenny Carpenter, who had left Vesterton Comprehensive the year before Young Tom, and worked in the small primary school in Leaf Street.

'Sergeant Wilson said there weren't no tracks leading out of the field – even stranger,' replied Jenny with a frightened shudder, tossing her long brown hair back over her shoulders. Handsome Young Tom had promised her a ride in his fast car as soon as he got it, and had stroked her arm as he said it. Now it didn't look as if Young Tom would keep his promise.

'Be a job for them Guardians,' said old Mrs Uttley, leaning across her cauliflowers to join in. 'Them that's supposed to help out when bad stuff happens.' Professor

Hullart turned on his heel and stooped to examine her carrots, listening intently. His unease had turned into a horrible certainty.

'Garn!' scoffed Tim Pritchett. 'Ain't no Guardians no more, surely. Reckon it's something to do with those posh student friends of Young Tom's. Them that came into the pub a sixmonth back, just after he went to Oxenfoord.' He grinned, thinking of Young Tom's embarrassment when all the drinkers in the Wyrm's Head had turned their backs and ignored the outsiders. They'd soon left, saying how bored they were. Luckily it hadn't been a night when the landlord was serving Merrilin Perry's Monster Brew. Although he reckoned a nice pair of horns apiece would have suited the posh gits nicely. Then he shivered. Wasn't lucky to scoff at things like the Guardians. Not in Wyrmesbury. Just in case. And certainly not with what might have happened that morning.

'My old great-grandma told me them Guardians stopped trouble hundreds of years back,' muttered Mrs Uttley obstinately. 'Stands to reason some of 'em 'ld still be about somewhere if needed in an odd ol' place like Wyrmesbury is.' She looked about to see if there were any outsiders about and mumbled in a low voice, 'You know. Real magic and all that – not just Merrilin's fun with the beer.'

Tim Pritchett coughed into the appalled silence that followed this normally forbidden topic. 'Well, that mist was odd . . . not to mention that we're gettin' more shakes than normal. And the hootcats were ever so noisy last night too. Maybe it'd be a good thing if them Guardians did turn up right about now. Make us all feel . . . safer somehow.' He turned and noticed Professor Hullart, still lurking among the vegetables. 'Now, Professor, how about a nice bag of Mrs Uttley's carrots to go with your cheese, and some of my best bacon?' he said, hurriedly changing the subject to something more normal.

Clutching several packages now, Professor Hullart walked on, trying to remember. There *had* been a lot of gossip six months before, when Young Tom had inherited the farm from his father.

Yes, that was right, old Tom had died of a sudden river ague, along with his wife and two elder sons. Only Young Tom and his younger sister Magret were left of the family, and she was still a schoolgirl, albeit a clever one who had set up quite a good little business on the side collecting the eggs from her hens for Mrs Huggins to sell at the market. So Young Tom was on his own, to do as he willed, master and farmer at just sixteen. The farm would have run itself, with a little care, and given just enough to keep both him and his sister, but Young Tom wanted more. Free from old Tom's mean restrictions, he could put in two old cousins to manage the place and look after Magret, and follow his dream of an Oxenfoord degree.

Soon people had begun whispering. They said that Young Tom was spending money like water, and that the farm coffers were emptying fast. That was the Wyrmesbury gossip anyway, and Professor Hullart saw no reason to disbelieve it.

But Professor Hullart was no ordinary man, and he knew bad news when he heard it. Young Tom meddling with Black Meadows was the worst news possible. And now Mrs Utley was talking about magic and she and Tim Pritchett and all the rest were talking about the Guardians again, which was a bigger worry still. No one in Wyrmesbury was supposed to talk about magic or even remember that the Guardians existed – except as some kind of amusing old wives' tale from the long ago past – let alone say that they'd feel safer with some around, unless there was real trouble brewing.

It was just like no one was able to look at Hootcat Hill for too long. There was a kind of old forgetting spell around Wyrmesbury, the seven hills and the Ash Valley that protected everyone from seeing or thinking about things that were better left alone.

He sighed and settled his grubby and battered tweed hat more firmly on his bald head as he trudged along the twisted streets and up to the old library. He felt suddenly ancient and tired and rather afraid. Surely the worldwyrm couldn't be wakening in his time. But he very much feared that it was. And that meant that Linnet Perry must be awakened to her Maiden Power.

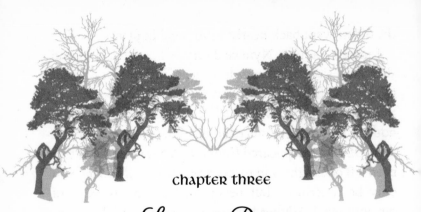

chapter three

Linnet Perry

Technomagic *(n.) (1) May also be known as
Technowyzardry (rare archaic usage). Used by the
non-scientific community to describe the workings of
such technological machinery as, for instance,
Medipods, where the techno-scientific explanation is
not readily understood by the lay community. (2) Sl.
term used to explain odd physical effects caused by
consumption of some man-made foods and drinks
(esp beers). (3) Events caused by humans that
are not explicable by normal scientific rules.
(Unscientific, unproven)*

From 'Dictionary of Applied Chymistry,
Technology and Physicks'

Linnet Perry and her parents lived in one of the
newer cottages in the town, down on the eastern
edge of Wyrmesbury. Newer was a relative term,
because no house in Wyrmesbury could really be called
new at all. They were all over a hundred years old, and

the oldest went back nearly a thousand in places.

Linnet's mother Nyneve Perry, who was small and slim with silver eyes and long dark hair, had not been born in the town and always said (slightly scornfully) that Wyrmesbury was stuck in a time warp, where nothing had changed since the last century or even before that. Objects disappeared from the places where they had been left one night, and reappeared the next in what could only be described (but never was) as an outbreak of outright magic. Other happenings, such as wild animals walking quietly down the streets in broad daylight; or eerie wind storms blowing up out of a clear blue sky were so common as not even to be worth a mention by Wyrmesbury dwellers. The frequent earth tremors were inconvenient to the china, but the townsfolk were quite used to them too, and tended to brush away any stray outsiders' questions rather brusquely, followed by muttered remarks about 'daft folk', who 'should mind they own business an' let ours alone'. Privately, of course, they were really rather proud of their town's odd reputation and resigned to its quirky weather patterns. Certainly they would never have considered living anywhere else. Wyrmesbury was how it was, and even if people did start to think about the underlying strangeness in more detail, the forgetting magic soon did its job of making their minds drift off to a different subject.

Linnet's father, Merrilin, *had* been born in Wyrmesbury – indeed Perrys had lived there for centuries, and were reputed to have wyzard blood. He was a thin, lanky man, with an untameable mop of dark red hair, and fingers stained from earth and from his hobby of brewing what he called 'experimental beers'. He was considered an odd character even by the town's rather liberal standards, and was therefore himself counted as part of the strangeness.

Since he spent most of his spare time encamped permanently in a damp mouldy cellar dabbling with technomagic this was not a surprise to anyone who knew him well. And when they took into account the slightly magical effects his Monster Brews had on those of the Wyrmesbury inhabitants who were brave enough to drink them in the local pub (usually late at night when other beers seemed unexciting), it was not surprising that most Wyrmesbury people were wary of Merrilin Perry's concoctions. Horns could normally be hidden under a hat until they wore off (about three hours later), but fangs were harder to conceal (and even harder to eat with), and it was almost impossible to stuff a particularly fine forked tail down the back of a pair of jeans, however baggy. Still, the folk of Wyrmesbury were tolerant of their own breed – especially one who came from a family as old and respected as the Perrys – and the landlord of the Wyrm's Head was wise enough not to let outsiders buy Merrilin's beer under any circumstances.

He and Linnet's mother had a small gardening business together, and as is the way with gardeners, their house was untidily crammed to bursting with rescued plants which seemed to thrive on little or no tending.

After she had turned off the alarm, Linnet got dressed in her school uniform and went past the thirty spider plants with their hundred babies and down the curling wooden stairs to the kitchen. The third step from the bottom creaked and whined secrets at her as usual. Smells of slightly burnt bacon and toast wafted towards her as she opened the door and saw her mother. Nyneve Perry smiled abstractedly at Linnet as she loaded a full plate and put it on the table in front of her. Linnet surreptitiously scraped the burnt bits off the toast – her mum was a really bad cook, but she didn't like it when anyone complained. Then she rolled her eyes and groaned as Nyneve looked over and said, 'Dad'll be up in a minute – he's just checking the latest Monster Brew.'

Dad was embarrassingly obsessed with his hobby. But it was always fun going with him to find the more exotic ingredients he put in his brews, and she loved mixing them up with him. She'd even made a few suggestions for Brews herself, which he said had turned out astonishingly well, and that she was going to be a natural at it when she was older. That had made her feel good about herself for once. She couldn't wait till she was old enough to go to the pub and see the effects. Linnet was quite comfortable with that kind of technomagic. It was funny and fairly harmless. She wasn't so sure about the other magic stuff, like the seeing colours round people. She suspected her dad's friend Wayland could see them too, but when she'd asked him about it the other day, he had just laughed, and told her not to be silly.

The stuff that frightened her most of all, though, were the all-too-real wyrm nightmares that came more and more often, sometimes even breaking into her mind in the daytime. Those weren't funny at all when she thought about them too hard. Young Tom's terrified, shrieking face flashed in her mind again, and she pushed her plate away, feeling sick.

She wiped her mouth hurriedly and got up from the table, grabbing her schoolbag from the dresser. The awful Frankish test, Geography, Physicks, English today – at least it was Shakspear which was the only thing she really enjoyed – and in the afternoon the dreaded games where she always got picked last for the team and kicked whenever the teacher wasn't looking. Linnet sighed and hitched the bag onto her shoulder. As she did so, a warning blue flicker – a flicker with wings – caught her eye from the corner of the room, and almost immediately the dresser began to shake and dance across the stone floor. Linnet clutched her head and screamed silently. Searing colours shivered in front of her – more nightmares of flame and blackness and teeth and red eyes with slanted golden pupils. Then the vision and the shaking were gone as suddenly as they had come and everything was normal again.

Linnet picked her way across a wreckage of fallen chairs to her mother, who stood in the midst of a mess of broken blue and white china, listening intently. She didn't notice Linnet's distress. As usual, thought Linnet, a flow of bitterness overwhelming her for a moment. It's always Dad she looks for first when there's trouble. Never me. And she gets upset when I even mention seeing colours round people, so a dragon vision would probably freak her out completely. No wonder it's impossible for me to tell her what's going on at school. Almost at once the cellar door banged open and a man erupted into the room, rumpled red hair standing on end, his hands cradling a demijohn which fizzed angrily. Merrilin Perry rushed over to his wife and daughter.

'Another earth tremor,' he said. 'I just managed to save the Brew.' Then he shook himself as if remembering something and set the demijohn down carefully on the table. 'Are you both all right?' he asked more mildly.

'I think so, dear,' said Nyneve. 'The casserole dish nearly fell on my head, and all the best blue plates broke, but I think so. What about you, Linnet?' she added as an afterthought.

Linnet wasn't at all sure that she was all right, but she also didn't think she was going to say so. Instead she just nodded silently. Her father looked at her suspiciously – he was not fooled. He never was.

'Hmmn,' he said. 'I wonder . . .' But what he wondered about he did not say, because the cuckoo clock on the wall chimed a quarter-to-eight just then and it was time for her to leave for school.

'Better check the street for damage,' said Merrilin, going to the front door. 'This one was even stronger than last night's.'

Linnet shivered. So she hadn't imagined being shaken out of her bed – and if she hadn't imagined that, then the dragon might be true too.

The three of them looked out of the door and up the street to see if the neighbours were all right. John the postman was delivering letters two houses up and Wyrmesbury life seemed to be carrying on as normal, despite the disruption of a few fallen tiles. Linnet picked up her bag again, waved to her parents and set out for the bus stop.

'Don't forget we'll be out very late at the plant fair

tonight, Linnet,' called her mother. 'Don't wait up for us.' Linnet nodded as she shouted goodbye and ran down the hill towards the bus stop on the main road. Her heart sank as she remembered again that today there was no Petroc to protect her from Them. At least, she'd have Magret Bickerspike to walk into school with. She hoped. If her dream about Young Tom had been just a dream.

chapter four

Visions in the Water, Signs in the Air

. . . ye may see the past in the seeing bowl
with eyebright herb both dried and whole . . .

from 'Eolin's Herbal for Seers'

*A*fter his usual struggle with the key to the locked case at the back marked 'Strictly No Admittance to the Public', Professor Hullart dug out the manuscript written by Hullavick the Historian which dealt with Wyrmesbury happenings from before the time his grandfather's father's grandfather was born. This was a document the general population of Wyrmesbury were definitely not encouraged to look at. He adjusted his glasses on his beaky nose and began to read . . .

On the sixteenthe day of September, in the yeare Fifteen Hundred and Thirty Three, there came a great shaking of the earthe under Wyrmesbury and a great wind came out of the sky and blasted the vallye below, and the people of the towne were sore afraid and barricaded themselves in their houses for they were feared that the Godde One had turned his face from them.

And the people of the vallye told afterwardes of greedy folk from outside who dug for some treasure they had heard of in the fields which the superstitious among us name as Black Meadowes. And they said that the Fey Folk came at the sound of digging and danced around those who dug, and that the noise of their stamping feet woke a great Wyrm who was roused up and ate up the treasure seekers, so that they were never again seen among us. And those same superstitious folk also spoke in whispers of the duty of the Guardians to protect the towne as they ever had before in troublous times when magick broke through the barriers set upon it, and of all manner of goddeless, pagan prophecies of the Maiden who should save us all. And Father Paul our priestman had to speak sternly of such ungoddeliness among us, and chastise those who spoke so with penances great and small . . .

from 'Ye Historie of Wyrmesbury 1564'

Professor Hullart sighed, rolled up the manuscript carefully, and set it back in its locked case. It was just as he had feared – or worse.

He closed the library again and walked down Wychbold Street to the chymist's shop. It was a high stone building, with mossy gables and a large bow-fronted window containing huge old-fashioned decanters of red and green liquid, topped by pointed glass stoppers which caught the light. Also contained in the window were piles of pale-coloured soaps and a wooden chest with a series of small drawers, each labelled in spidery brown writing with names such as Astralagus, Serpent Stones, Bogbean, Helleborine, Onion, Tormentil and Yarrow. He opened the door, over which was written, 'F. Morgan. B.Chym. B. Hom, Herbalist' and went in. A bell tinkled loudly over his head.

Behind the counter stood a short, plump lady of indeterminate age. Her hair was pure white and piled on top of her head in a neat double bun like a cottage loaf. She had smooth rosy cheeks and deep violet-coloured eyes which were hidden at the moment behind a pair of half moon spectacles. She was wearing a white chymist's coat.

As the bell rang, she looked up to see who had come in. She smiled at the Professor briefly, then went on serving a young woman with a baby. He sighed impatiently, and moved over to the counter, willing the chymist to hurry.

'Two packets of nappies and some gripe water, please,' said the young woman, whose baby was now starting to cry. 'He's teething something awful, Miss Morgan.'

'Then you don't need gripe water,' said the chymist firmly, rummaging under the counter and digging out a small packet and a tube of gel. 'Try him on some of this chamomile tea, warm, four times a day. And rub some of this gel on his poor little gums.'

'Thanks ever so much, Miss Morgan,' said the young woman. She shifted uncomfortably and leaned over the counter to whisper. 'I'll need one of your specials too. Brian went and drank one of Merrilin's Brews at the pub and now he's got *talons*. He can't get a pair of shoes on for love nor money.'

The chymist laughed. 'That'll teach him!' she said. 'Give him a drop of what I gave you last time. Only a drop, mind you. They should wear down in a few hours or so.'

As soon as she had gone, Fay Morgan hurried across to the door, locked it, and turned the sign on it to 'Closed'.

'Did you feel it, Tyto?' she asked the Professor urgently. 'Did you feel the worldwyrm move last night? And have you heard the gossip about Young Tom Bickerspike?'

Professor Hullart nodded slowly. 'I felt it last night and again this morning. And I've been down to the marketplace and listened to Mrs Huggins, and Tim Pritchard and all of them gossiping. Apart from Young Tom and Black Meadows, which is bad enough, they're also talking about the Guardians and fairies, and stuff they've no business even remembering exists, if the spells are working right. Stuff that their ancestors last thought about nearly five hundred years ago. I've just been and looked it all up in the old histories. I'm afraid the wind messages have been right in their warnings this spring, but we still need to find out what really happened down at Bickerspike's Farm last night.'

'Can we do it with just Two?' she asked.

Professor Hullart closed his eyes for a moment. 'I don't think so,' he said. 'We'll need the Smith to hold the energy while we Two watch what went on. I shall summon him at once.' He delved about in his trouser pocket and brought out a silver talisman shaped like a hootcat owl, with outspread wings. He took it in his left hand and stared at it with eyes, which, when you looked at them in a certain light seemed round and golden and not quite human. His lips moved.

'Wayland Smith, you are summoned by need,' he muttered. Then again, and louder. 'Wayland Smith, you are summoned by need.' The silver owl lay mute and dead in his hand, and Professor Hullart looked up at Fay Morgan. 'Blast and bother him,' he growled. 'When he's in that workshop of his tinkering with cars and engines, he's oblivious to everything. I shall have to use the emergency call, and if it burns him then too bad.'

The school bus was later than usual and full of chatter. Normally Linnet would have sat with Petroc, despite the whoops and catcalls from the other boys, who respected Petroc for his size and ability at football, but couldn't understand why he liked a stupid girl. He had been her best friend since the day they started together at the primary school in Leaf Street, and Linnet was thankful for it. Her life would have been a lot harder without him.

As the bus rumbled slowly down its usual route and along the valley to Vesterton, her mind turned to the day ahead, and her heart gave a jolt as she wondered where exactly They would be waiting for her, and what They would do to her. Linnet sat quietly on her own at the back, away from the small, squabbling herd of Wyrmesbury boys. She made herself stop thinking about Them, and thought instead about the next stop, where Magret Bickerspike would be getting on.

Linnet admired Magret. She'd come through a lot. First

her dad had died of the river ague. Nobody had been too sorry about that, because he was a mean and surly man, with a reputation of being cruel to his family. Magret told Linnet privately that he sometimes hit her for no reason other than that she was a girl. But then her two eldest brothers had died – and worst of all, her mum had caught the ague and died too – worn to the bone with nursing them all. Only Magret, the youngest, and Young Tom had escaped.

Magret was pretty (when she could be bothered to dress up), intelligent, and more importantly she was the only other girl anywhere nearby who was close to Linnet's age, and so they were friends of a sort, even though Magret was two classes above, and Linnet didn't see much of her in school. Apart from helping with torn books and stuff, Magret was almost as good as Petroc at cheering Linnet up when They had been really vile.

Now that her parents were gone, sometimes she invited Linnet for tea, or to stay the night. Magret's father had never allowed her to have friends round – he had made Magret work in the dairy or the henhouse, and in those days she'd never had pretty dresses like she did now. Her father had made her wear cast-offs from the charity shop because he said he couldn't afford to buy her new clothes.

Young Tom had changed all that for his sister when he'd inherited the farm and started spending money like water. Linnet smiled to herself soppily. She especially liked going to the Bickerspike house when Young Tom was home. He had an aura of danger and glamour about him that she found made her go all funny in the pit of her stomach. And he was always nice to her, teasing her and making her blush with his jokes, though Magret seemed rather jealous when he did that, and tended to whisk her upstairs rather quickly. Then her heart gave another jolt as she remembered her dream. What if Magret didn't turn up? Then she'd have to believe all that horrible stuff she'd dreamed about Young Tom was true. She suddenly felt sick to her stomach.

As they passed the Bickerspike Farm entrance, the bus slowed and stopped as it usually did. Magret Bickerspike was nowhere to be seen, only a man standing by a small red car and speaking urgently into a technophone, together with several police cars parked up the farm road. The man on the technophone looked cross and worried. The bus driver waited for a while, cursed and drove on. Linnet clenched her fists, as she realised that her nightmare had come true. If the police were around and Magret was not coming to school, it definitely meant something really bad had happened at Bickerspike's Farm. Young Tom was always on at Magret to work hard and use her brains even though he seemed oddly against her trying for the University — she had never missed school, not even once since her parents had died.

Linnet shivered and closed her eyes, thinking again of the way Young Tom's face had been in her nightmare. He hadn't looked at all handsome, screaming. Colours started to swirl behind her eyelids and she hurriedly opened them and stared fixedly ahead at the disgusting brownish-orange pattern, sticky with old gum, on the furry seat back in front of her and firmly thought of nothing at all. So she didn't see the unusual pearly mist swirling and whirling over Black Meadows as the bus passed by, nor, ten minutes later did she notice the police cars rushing back towards Vesterton, overtaking on the wrong side of the road, blue lights flashing.

Vesterton's untidy modern sprawl covered half of the valley six miles to the north of Wyrmesbury, beyond the stone quarries at High Furling. It was surrounded by industrial estates full of tall brick chimneys whose dirty smoke could be seen rising up even against the greyest sky. Vesterton Comprehensive lay slumped in the middle of the town – a mess of concrete and cracked glass and graffiti and temporary classrooms which were always going to be replaced by the government of the day and never were. Linnet hated it with a passion. But there was nowhere else for the Wyrmesbury children to go once they had finished at the tiny primary school in Leaf Street.

Everyone piled off the bus, running and shouting. Linnet followed, dragging unwilling feet. She knew what was bound to happen sooner or later and she groaned as she turned the corner to her classroom and saw Them waiting.

'Ooh! It's the weirdo of Wyrmesbury!' said the worst of Them – a thin, mean-eyed girl called Lellicia Sundew. 'And just look – she hasn't got Boy Wonderful to protect her today, or her big clever girlfriend either! Why not give her a pinch and a punch for the first of the month? It's a day early, but we can give her another one tomorrow.'

Linnet walked on through the jeers and catcalls of the others, ignoring Them. It was the only thing she could think of to do. As she passed, fat, spotty Robert Bowker spat at her feet, and Tony Skink tried to jerk the schoolbag off her shoulder. The rest closed in and surrounded her in a tight, threatening, snarling semi-circle, which drew in nearer and nearer. Needless to say, there were no teachers around, just when she needed one. They were probably all drinking coffee in the staffroom, putting off seeing their horrible pupils till the last possible moment. She didn't blame them. She turned, her back to the classroom door, and glared at Them miserably, fending off the mean punching and pinching with her hands and feet as best she could. Her eyes felt hot and gritty, and then suddenly out of the corners she could see blue wings flickering and flashing for the second time that day.

Her heart was thudding its way out of her chest, her throat had gone dry and tight with absolute terror at what might happen if she looked. But she was starting to lose the battle. Clumps of her hair were being pulled out and so she gritted her teeth and dared herself to stare directly at the shapes between the bright blue wings. Linnet gave a small, panicked gasp as she saw tiny, fierce looking creatures, each carrying a sharp spear, and dressed in what looked like moss and leaves. Then she began to hear a faintly aggressive buzz above the jeering voices. It sounded oddly comforting.

'Help!' she whispered to the nearest. 'Help me – please!' And suddenly the buzz grew to a frantic hum, and They began to slap at their arms and legs as the winged creatures pricked at them with their spears.

'What? . . . Who's doing that? . . . Gerroff . . .' They

cried. And seconds later Linnet had the satisfaction of seeing Them run off down the corridor as if pursued by an invisible swarm of angry wasps, just as the bell rang and Mr Snawkins the Frankish teacher came round the corner, wiping coffee off his moustache.

'No running in the corridors!' he yelled automatically. Linnet grinned and walked into class.

'Thanks,' she whispered to the air.

Just inside her head came a chorus of tiny buzzing voices. 'Today we are the Protectors of Linnet the Maiden. No thanks are needed.'

Linnet was beyond blinking now. Too many strange things had happened already today for her to be surprised at one more, and she was too grateful for their unexpected help to argue with her winged saviours. But she did wonder if they had somehow got her mixed up with someone else. Some Maiden person who had fairy protectors. Then she remembered the badger that morning. He too had greeted her as Linnet the Maiden. And she was supposed to go and visit him tonight. How was that going to fit in with homework?

She shook her head and settled down to concentrate on Mr Snawkins, who was chalking up irregular Frankish verbs on the blackboard for the test. The letters went wiggly and strange and danced around her eyes, as they always seemed to, but she willed them into order and started to scribble furiously, if inaccurately.

'*Aller* – to go,' she muttered. '*J'alais* . . .' Blue fairy-things and Maidens and talking badgers would just have to wait till school was over.

*

On the other side of Wyrmesbury from Fay Morgan's shop, a man stood in a dark garage, surrounded by metal panels and tools and anonymous vehicle parts. A gigantic forge stood in one corner of the building, glowing dully red. The man was dressed in huge oil-stained blue overalls, a welding mask covered his face and a stream of blue and gold sparks streamed from his hand onto the piece of metal he was welding. He was nearly seven feet tall, with the thick muscles that denote immense strength, and he was humming tunelessly as he worked. Suddenly the sparks died, and he clapped a hand to his broad backside. A red glow showed through the material of the pocket and it began to smoke.

'Need Call answered,' he yelled, fumbling at the pocket, and the red glow extinguished itself immediately. The man drew out a small silver anvil and looked at it disgustedly. 'I felt you the first time,' he said to it grumpily. 'Just wanted to finish that panel. There wasn't any need to use the emergency.'

Professor Hullart's voice came out of the anvil, tinny and disembodied.

'Fay and I need you right now to hold the energy for a Seeing. The Bickerspike boy has disappeared in Black Meadows, the wyrm has moved and the town is talking of Guardians again. Don't you hear anything from that forge of yours, Wayland?'

Wayland Smith grunted. He did hear – sort of – but he wasn't one to panic over Wyrmesbury gossip, especially when it concerned that Bickerspike lad who was always on at him to soup up some old car to go as fast as the ones his posh friends owned. 'I'm on my way,' he said.

Five minutes later there was a roar of blue exhaust outside the chymist's shop as a flame-red motorbike came to a screeching halt outside the door. The handle rattled loudly as Fay came out to unlock it, and Wayland Smith entered, bending his head to avoid the tinkling bell.

'Come into the back, Wayland,' she said. 'Everything is nearly ready for the Seeing. I just need to set it up.'

She drew him swiftly into the back room behind the curtain that divided her home from the shop, then went to a cupboard and brought out a low silver dish which she set on a table, then filled with water. Professor Hullart greeted Wayland with a curt nod, and gestured to a chair.

'Eyebright,' muttered Fay, rummaging through the small jars that littered the room. 'Where did I put the eyebright and the eelfoot oil?'

Moments later the Three of them were seated around the dish, staring into the water in which specks of herb floated amongst oily swirls of purple, sweet-smelling ink. They began to chant.

> *Ola cas easgainn*
> *Ann an Adharc muice glan*
> *Open our eyes with the eyebright weed,*
> *Eelfoot oil and fleafat weed*
> *To See the parts of the past that we need.*

The surface of the inky water began to swirl and smoke and both Fay Morgan and Professor Hullart stifled a cry as they heard and Saw and smelt . . .

*

The summer mist swirled around the lower valley as the technomachine arrived on its transporter and was lowered slowly down by the top gateway. The technomachine operator's small red car was parked on the roadside verge, and he waved goodbye to the transporter driver as he drove back towards the industrial estate at Vesterton. Young Tom Bickerspike stuck his hands in his overalls and whistled as he watched the technomachine move slowly over the fields towards the river. A great yellow monster it seemed, looming and booming on its revolving caterpillar feet, with a huge drill poking out of its head like a giant horn.

'Come to make my fortune,' he whispered greedily.

The water swirled and turned again, and they Saw a different picture . . .

Down in the bottom left-hand corner of the farm were two fields that had never been touched with a plough. Boggy they were, and full of a black mud that stank of burning brimstone and shone with strange rainbow colours in the sun. A small boy stood there with his father.

'Why don't we plough these, Dad?' he asked. ''Tis rich soil, surely?'

'We leave 'em fer the Fey Folk,' said Old Tom Bickerspike. 'Bad luck to touch Black Meadows. It's said there's somewhat underneath 'em that don't like being disturbed. Times past there've been them from outside that tried, and it never came to a good end. Leave 'em alone, boy. The rest of the land provides enough.' . . .

The picture changed again and again, swift glimpses of different scenes, always with Young Tom Bickerspike at the centre and Wayland Smith groaned with the effort of holding the energy that was needed to keep the spell steady.

Young Tom arguing with his father, a letter in his hand with the crest of Oxenfoord University on it . . .

'No Bickerspike has ever gone to study in the University, and you shan't neither. Farm's good enough for me, and it'll be good enough for you.'

'You'll not stop me studying Chymistry, Dad, not with the scholarship money come through . . .'

'Over my dead body, boy . . .'

Scenes of funerals and a weeping Magret held up by her brother. Then Young Tom standing by Black Meadows gathering test tubes full of the strange mud as it glopped and oozed and made strange muffled roaring noises around him . . .

Young Tom standing by a man in a white coat in a laboratory . . .

'Black gold, Mr Bickerspike. That's what you've got here. Invaluable to the technomagicians, and worth a fortune to any man who takes the time and trouble to drill it out of the ground . . .'

Young Tom looking on enviously as his rich student friends drove their fast cars and laughed with the shiny girls that wealth brought them. Then back to the first picture again.

'Black gold,' Young Tom muttered to the fields as he

watched the technomachine approach. 'Black gold you are, and all mine.' The ground shuddered and bucked under his feet as he spoke, but he took no notice, thinking it was only the vibration of the technomachine.

Fay Morgan and Professor Hullart saw all of what followed, and shuddered together as the red catlike eyes slipped back into the mud, and they smelt the failed magic in the pearly Fey mist that rose above the worldwyrm's bed. They saw the police who had come when called by the technomachine operator that same morning and took notes and scratched their heads, and they saw Young Tom's sister Magret dry-eyed and angry as she was questioned over and over about her brother. They heard the technomachine operator babbling of strange-coloured green mists and stubborn levers that yesterday had not turned as they should. But now there was no technomachine in Black Meadows, no sign of Young Tom Bickerspike – only dragging caterpillar tracks that led into the field but not out of it, and then disappeared into nothing as the vision faded.

Fay looked across the now still water at Professor Hullart and Wayland Smith, and her rosy face was pale with worry and strain.

'It is a full moon and Beltain Eve tonight, the time when the old magic and our Powers become strongest. It is clear that the Fey Folk and their Queen have danced their warning and that the worldwyrm has indeed been awoken by Young Tom Bickerspike's greedy meddling.

'There is no help for it, Linnet Perry must be summoned into her full Power as the Maiden at once. We will need all the strength of Seven Guardians to make the wyrm sleep truly deep again, as well as that of the Fey Queen and her people, if they can be persuaded – which is doubtful, given the circumstances of their binding and punishment. We just have to hope it will be satisfied by its meal last night, and that the Fey have succeeded in making it sleep lightly again for a while.'

Professor Hullart nodded slowly. 'Nearly five hundred years,' he said bitterly. 'Nearly five hundred years since the worldwyrm last awoke. Things have changed a bit since then. Beltain Eve or not, all our Powers have been weakened by this modern world, and I fear our efforts will prove to be in vain. The old magic has had its day. But we are bound to try, for Linnet's sake if nothing else.' He sighed. 'Poor child, all this will come as a terrible shock to her. Especially finding out that those of us who have been close to her and her family have been so for reasons other than friendship.'

'Linnet is a lot tougher than you might think,' said Fay Morgan. 'Just look at how hard she's worked at her reading problems with you. And I've a strong suspicion she may have inherited a talent for Merrilin's technomagic – I've seen the instinctive way she mixes ingredients for him without even thinking about it. She will surprise all of us, I'm sure. But you are right, we must all do what we can to hold the wyrm back till she is ready. You are closest to the badger. Tell Sunstar he must bring Linnet to your Owlstones on Hootcat Hill before moonrise. We will be waiting for her.'

The Professor nodded again. 'He will already realise what is happening, but I will go to the mound anyway and consult with him before he takes his nap,' he said. 'The badger folk keep all the Guardian lore. He is the one who told us of her birth thirteen years ago, and so he must be the one who starts her Awakening. But there is so little time for him to teach her what she needs to know.'

Wayland chuckled, the deep sound lightening the rather gloomy atmosphere. 'Oh, I don't know. Linnet's always had some idea that she's different, I reckon. Haven't you ever noticed her watching the colours round people? I've caught her at it a few times. I've never told her I can see them too, of course, though she asked me the other day. What she has to do is really very simple – she just has to accept her Power, and after that her Maiden memories will help her. Fay's right – I think you should trust her instincts. She'll surprise us all.'

Professor Hullart looked at him open-mouthed. 'Simple?' he said. 'Simple? Let me remind you what she has to do, Wayland. This child, who will, if all goes well, be newly come to the ways of magic, has to find her way into the otherworld of Avvallon – the land of the Fey Folk and their Queen, who, let me remind you, are never too well-disposed to Maidens. The Fey Queen *really* hates being made to guard that wyrm, and she sees it all as the Maiden's fault. Getting her through the Door to Avvallon is my job, but I cannot do it without the help of her own Power, which she does not yet have, and if and when she does will have very little time to learn to use. Then she has to somehow avoid any traps that Fidget Reedglitter and the Fey Prince set for her in Avvallon – or worse still, capture – seek out the no doubt well-hidden Chalice of Athyr and steal it. On top of that, she also has to find and bring back to this mortal world the dragonwort elixir that is the only thing which will send the worldwyrm back to sleep, and pour it down the beast's throat. Simple? I'd like to see you try it. And you are old and wise in the ways of magic.'

Wayland Smith grinned. 'Thanks for the compliment, Prof. I shall have to remember how old and wise I am next time you burn my backside with a Need Call. Now, if we're all finished here, I've got a panel to finish beating. Owlstones at moonrise it is,' he said, rising to go. 'See you there.' The door slammed behind him and soon the roar of a powerful motorbike disturbed the quiet streets of Wyrmesbury once more.

chapter five

The Calling of the Maiden

First comes Rhiannon, daughter of Mares,
Second the Wyccan, brightweaver of Airs.
Third comes the Staghorned, he of the Chase.
Fourthly the Owlman whose Stones wear his face.
Fifth comes the Badger, sunmarked at birth,
Sixth is the Smith bringing Fire from Earth.
Six guard the town in the time of Its sleep,
But Seven must rise when Wyrm stirs in the deep . . .

from 'The Prophecies of the Seven'

*T*he white mare had been restless since morning. She roamed the slopes of Rinnon's Crest, sniffing at the late evening air and watching the dewmist swirl and rise around her silver hooves.

Oldest of all the Guardians, born a long ago time, she was uneasy and afraid. The wind had been bringing her messages of change and great danger all that spring, and now her nostrils prickled and burned with warnings that smelt like fire and darkness. Why could she not see the pattern in this at once as she used to centuries before? She answered herself immediately. This modern sort of human had become too strong. The balance was tipping away from the old magic, and her ancient Power had waned from what it was. In these present times humans, and the new kind of Power called technomagic with its machines that flew and its strange, soulless metal contraptions ruled, not the old natural magic that she knew best. Only at dawn and evening shade was she now visible at all in any form, and only at dawn and by moonlight could she work her own magic truly.

She galloped to the top of the hill and looked out over the valley beneath and the seven hills surrounding it in a protective circle, of which her own was the southernmost. Her eyes passed over Wyrmesbury in the centre, yellow lights twinkling from the ancient town spread over its massive slopes, past Cerne Tump, and Forge Highers, over Maiden's Mount and Witches Tor and finally to the sugarloaf shape of Hootcat Hill. She whinnied quietly as she felt the throbbing force of the magic Owlstone circle on its summit, hidden by the deep spellmist and thickets of green trees. Underneath them lay hidden the Door to Avvallon, land of the Fey Folk. Galloping fast, the mare soon stood beside the stones, each carved with the figure of a hootcat owl.

The River Ash wound around the seven hills and through the valley in a great loop, flowing past Cerne Tump to the west, and then turning north towards Vesterton as it ran through Black Meadows. Its waters flared white in the first rays of a late moonrise, and the mare stiffened as the moonlight hit the Owlstones and finally, finally, she saw the pattern which glowed and whirled and settled in the meadow on the other side of the river as its mad spiralling green dance of warning ended. She drew in a deep, snorting breath as she felt the earth trembling and shaking under her hooves, called on the moon's Power, and Changed.

Standing in the mare's stead amid the mists at the top of Hootcat Hill was a slender, beautiful woman, tall and stately with a chain of moondaisies threaded through her long silver hair. She pulled her golden cloak about her and shivered, though the night was not cold. Putting her fingers to her lips, she whistled a short burst of complicated notes that echoed oddly, as if they were coming from underground. There was a flutter of wings, and three birds appeared from the earth at her feet, and flew up to settle, one on each of her shoulders, and one on the top of her head.

'Greetings, little sisters,' she said aloud, and her voice was deep and hoarse with a hint of breathy whinny at its back.

The birds chirrupped and chattered and cooed, according to their natures, and it seemed that the woman could understand them, for she spoke again.

'Yes, it has been long and long since you were my eyes and ears, little sisters, but Rhiannon has need of each of you now, for the Fey Folk have danced a warning in Black Meadows, and the worldwyrm has risen from his lair. Morrina, my golden sparrow, fly for me now, and bring me news from all the Underdwellers, dwarf, and

Merr and Hulda and everything in between.' The small sparrow on her left shoulder circled her head before disappearing underground again.

'Mocker, my greenfinch, fly for me and bring me news of the Chalice of Athyr and the dragonwort elixir from the Fey Folk. But do not be seen – watch for the sorceress.' The emerald green finch on her right shoulder gave a trilling cry before following the sparrow.

'Bough, my white dove, you shall fly first to Cernunnos the Stagman, and tell him that I have finally read the pattern and that the Owlstones will see a meeting of the Seven on Beltain Eve. And then you shall go to the bluewinged Kobold and ask their leader Skystone to aid the human Maiden, Linnet Perry, who must Awaken now. Tell them to protect her wherever she goes tomorrow – I have seen that she will be attacked in some way. And also bid them escort her to the badger's lair before dusk tomorrow if they can. Human Maidens can be stubborn creatures, and they may need to use the compelling magic on her feet. For there are many things that she must learn from Sunstar before he brings her to the Guardians.'

The dove cooed and bent down, brushing her beak gently over Rhiannon's brow before flying off towards Cerne Tump, where the horned Stagman, Cernunnos, had his home, deep in a cave in the craggy fern-covered rocks that littered the eastern slope.

He was wearing his most human form when she found him, sitting at the cave entrance and snuffing at the night air. His hairy torso gleamed chestnut and gold in the moonlight, and his magnificent horns sprang from the hooded mask of green leaves and fern that covered his head and face. Bough swept down a moonbeam and landed on his shoulder.

'Ho! Small one! I smell news from Hootcat Hill!' he growled in a voice that belled and rang like thunder round the rocks.

'My mistress has read the pattern, and she bids you make yourself ready,' cooed the dove. 'You are summoned to a meeting.'

'So I felt truly, then. We must be Seven once more,' Cernunnos whispered softly, and the echoes of it hissed and whined around the rocks. He flexed his huge muscles under the shaggy pelt that covered him and shuddered. Rising from his mossy seat, he pounded on a rock with his great fist, striding about and striking sparks with his hooves. 'I have seen many Maidens over the centuries, and they are weak little things. Remember the last one? She who got caught and held by the Fey Folk and had to be rescued at great risk. What will this one be like? Weak and puny, no doubt, however special she is in other ways!' But Bough had no answer for him, and she flew off to summon Skystone and his troop of Blue Kobold to Linnet's aid.

Linnet thumped her schoolbag down on the kitchen table and went to the fridge, muttering crossly. She'd failed her Frankish test as usual, and games had been just as awful as she'd feared. One good thing had happened, though, she thought, looking down at her bruised legs and feeling her sore scalp. Not one of Them had managed to get any more sly kicks or pinches or hairpulls in. It was almost as if she'd had a protective wall round her, because every time They had moved in for the kill, something had simply prevented them from getting near. She hadn't seen the funny blue-winged creatures again, but maybe, just maybe she hadn't imagined them.

'Bet Mum's forgotten to get me cheese again as usual,' she said, slamming open the door so the milk bottles rattled. Mum had and there was only some old, dry ham curling at the corners, so Linnet had to do with four slices of toast, heavily buttered. Her mother was only ever practical when it came to looking after plants. Food came a very poor second to green things.

Juggling a plate, a glass of milk and her books, Linnet walked out to the garden to do her homework. Her parents wouldn't be home for hours and hours she remembered – so she curled up comfortably on the swing seat and settled down to learn her Frankish over again in the pale sunshine of late afternoon.

An hour later she was deep in a struggle to read about bauxite mines for her Geography lesson, when a buzz at her ear distracted her. She swatted at it irritably. It grew louder, with a slightly aggrieved tone to it. Linnet looked up. Hovering in front of her was a troop of the winged blue beings again.

'Hello,' she whispered. 'Who are you? And why are you here?' The biggest of them flew down and settled on the arm of the swing seat beside her. Linnet looked at him really properly for the first time. He had a blue triangular face, with a pointed chin and black bootbutton eyes that seemed to draw the light in and hold it. He had a double set of gauzy wings like a dragonfly's, and he wore a belt of shining blue stones around his leafy tunic.

'Hail, Linnet the Maiden,' he said in his high, buzzing voice. 'We are the Blue Kobold, the Protectors. I am Skystone, the leader. We have watched over you all today, as the Daughter of Mares instructed us, and now we have come to take you to the Guardian Sunstar, where you will learn things you need to know. Come!' He held out a small hand imperiously. 'Come now, the Daughter of Mares herself has commanded it.'

Linnet shut her eyes tight and then opened them again. Skystone and his troop were still there, so she couldn't be dreaming. She knew she ought to feel scared, but somehow she wasn't. She just felt rather obstinate about being told what to do by a load of blue midgets with wings. And who was this Daughter of Mares to command her, anyway?

'But . . .' she said rebelliously, 'I've still got home-work . . .'

'Come,' said Skystone again. 'The Daughter of Mares said you would be stubborn, but it is time.' He made a small, twisty gesture, and an amazed Linnet found herself up on her feet and walking behind him without knowing how she'd got there, or quite what had happened. The first evening dew was falling, and she smelt the sweet scent of the honeysuckle rising again as her feet took themselves forward past the blossoming apple trees, past the rows of feathery carrots just poking through the black soil of the vegetable garden and the untidy pea sticks with a few tentative green tendrils furling round them. She stumbled through the hole in the hedge, scratching herself badly, and moved down the field towards the old mound. Just as she reached it, Skystone poked his spear into a groove in a curiously carved rock. There was a brief blue shimmering, and then a low door appeared in the mound. There was a dark passage inside, and a smell emerged from it which reminded Linnet of old books which have gone slightly musty. It was very strong. Skystone and his troop fluttered inside, and slowly the passage brightened.

'Come,' they cried. 'Come before the door magic wanes.' So Linnet came, her insubordinate feet again leading her forward by some command other than her own. The passage walls were smooth and ancient, and there were pictures on them, pictures that woke strange memories, pictures that she almost knew the meaning of. She felt a great yearning inside to stop and study them, as if they would help her to make sense of everything that was happening to her.

'Stop,' she cried. 'Stop! I want to look.' But Skystone shook his head while his troop prodded her on and her disobedient feet followed despite her wishes, down down down, until she found herself in a large vaulted chamber. At the end of the chamber was a raised bed, covered with fresh green fronds of fern and bracken. On it stood a badger.

'Oh,' said Linnet in surprise, though surprise was now something that seemed to belong, like fear, to the world she had left outside. 'Oh! It's you!' The badger inclined his muzzle gravely, and his voice sounded inside her head for the second time that day.

'It is indeed me. Welcome to my home, Linnet the Maiden. I am Sunstar the Guardian, and many of your questions will be answered here. Come and sit by me, we have little time, and you have a story to hear before the moon rises.'

Linnet was bursting with curiosity, but she did as Sunstar said and made herself comfortable on the bracken beside him. Skystone and his troop fluttered into crevices in the walls, filling the cavern with a soft blue light.

'Long ago,' said the badger in his deep, rough voice. 'Long, long ago, the world was a place where magic ruled, and most humans were weak, frightened creatures who hid in caves and crude shelters, living by the rhythms of the seasons as we animals do, and worshipping magical beings of all kinds as gods – Fey Folk and elves and Merrfolk and Hulda, unicorns, shapeshifters, earthdemons, dwarves and many more – who spoke to them sometimes in dreams.'

'Like me,' said Linnet, interrupting. 'I've always had dreams where things speak to me.'

'I know you have,' said Sunstar. 'Sometimes it was me. But hush now, and listen. One day there came a different kind of human – a mischievous, inquisitive girl – who wanted more. She wanted to know the secret of the red-golden magic that came to her in her dreams. The want of it swept through all her sleeping and waking hours until she could almost feel its heat on her cold, shivering body as it lay on the damp ground. She went to the Dreamer – the wisewoman who kept the dreams of the people safe – and asked her what she knew of it.

'"It is a very terrible thing called Fire," the Dreamer said sharply. "And no good will come of your asking." But the girl pestered and wheedled, until finally the

Dreamer told her that Fire was kept by the magical dragon, the worldwyrm, whose body curled around the hot heart of the earth and protected it from harm.

'"He sleeps deep, very deep," she murmured softly to herself. "And the dreams of the people say he must sleep forever and ever and ever, or terrible things will happen."

'"Forever and ever," said the girl scornfully. "What is forever, but a word telling us to do nothing, to change nothing, to stay as we are, cold and hungry? I spit on forever." And she spat on the ground at the wisewoman's feet and ran away, kicking at bushes as she went.'

Linnet wriggled awkwardly. The bracken was prickly on the backs of her legs, and she didn't like this talk of magical dragons, but she had to know. She took a deep breath and interrupted the badger's story. 'I keep having dreams and visions about a . . . a . . . dragon – a wyrm,' she said quickly, before she could regret it. 'They're horrible. Is it this wyrm in the story?' Her voice faltered and went silent as a breath of red flame flashed before her eyes again. Sunstar brushed his head against her arm comfortingly.

'You are safe here,' he said, avoiding an answer, and went on with his story. 'Now the Fey Folk Queen, the dangerous and sly fairy who rules in Avvallon, had been out in the world with her people on their own wayward business when they heard the girl, and they determined to teach her a lesson. So as the girl ran, she found herself running down, down, on and on and on into a pit that had opened up in the earth. It was close and hot, and she had no light, but she was brave, if nothing else, and a thread of eerie music was drawing her on. Time meant nothing here as the Fey mischief lured her deeper – she could have been running for hours or days or years.

"'Maybe I can find this wyrm, and steal some of his Fire for myself,' said the girl, 'and then I can become a goddess too!' And indeed she grew more and more hopeful the deeper she went, because a red glow like the one in her dream began to show in the distance, and the heat was becoming unbearable. Suddenly the eerie music stopped, and she stumbled out into an enormous cave. There in front of her lay the head of a black wyrm, huger than the hugest mountain. Its body stretched far far back into the darkness, unimaginable in size and length. The wyrm's eyes were closed, and out of its nostrils trickled a thin but steady stream of smoke. Its head lay curled around a pool – a pool that glowed white-gold in the centre of a red hot bubbling mass that beat with a slow, steady rhythm. It was the earth's heart.

"'Fire!' breathed the girl. She reached into her pocket for a hollow reed which she had been making into a flute and started to climb up and over the wyrm's hot flank. As soon as the wyrm felt her feet, its eyes opened. They were a dark, shining red, with slitted golden pupils.

"'HAAAARHHHH!' it roared. And the wind of its breath sizzled and scorched the hair of the girl's head until she was quite bald, and quite naked too, for the fur of her tunic had burned away. She turned to run, but suddenly, out of the ground in front of her rose the shining, beautiful Fey Queen, pointed teeth bared, and hooked fingernails reaching for her. The music started up again and many Fey feet began to stamp and whirl in a mad dance of untamed wild faces, and long green hair flying. The wyrm opened its jaws and curled a long tongue round the girl's waist. She screamed and screamed as she went down the wyrm's long black throat, and then the screaming ended – cut off as suddenly as it had begun.'

'Stop!' shouted Linnet, her hands over her ears. 'That's just like my dream last night. How did you know? That's what's happened to poor Young Tom. The wyrm ate him the same as that girl.' She spun round and faced the badger on all fours, looking straight into his dark eyes, demanding answers, some of which she already knew deep inside herself. Sunstar sighed, a little impatiently.

'You must conquer your fear and hear the rest. Yes, you have seen Young Tom Bickerspike's fate, as you well know. We shan't get anywhere unless you believe what I am telling you beyond questioning,' he finished, rather severely Linnet felt. She subsided onto the bracken again, fists clenched and body braced to hear the end of the tale.

'The wyrm roared again,' continued the badger, 'and its head rose up out of the earth, which the Fey Queen and her people had not counted on at all when they lured the girl into its lair. It began to wreak havoc everywhere over the earth with its Fire, and not even the strong magic of the Fey Folk could stop it.'

Linnet stirred uncomfortably again. She didn't like where this story was going at all, but for the moment she said nothing, and listened intently.

'I said that most humans were poor, frightened creatures. But not all. Some humans had been taken by the Fey Queen as babies, and given magic Powers. The Fey Folk named the males as wyzards, and the females as wyccans. There weren't many – not more than two hundred or so of all ages – but they were all summoned with the rest to the great Meeting that was called to decide what must be done to put the wyrm to rest again.

'Much of what was said there it is not necessary to tell you. But in the end it was decided that since a human girl child had woken the dragon, the balance of magic demanded that a human girl child should put it to rest again. The arguments were very great, and many magics were cast to see the way forward, but in the end Rhiannon the Daughter of Mares, young though she was then, cried out that she had seen the pattern clear, and that there was a Maiden among the wyccans who could carry out the task.

> *"Behind her ear a triple mole*
> *and hair of white doth show.*
> *By these and eyes of blue and green*
> *The Maiden ye shall know . . ."*

sang Rhiannon's three birds, Mocker, Bough and Morrina. And those were the first words of the scrolls that we now call *The Prophecies of the Seven*.'

The badger glanced sideways at Linnet, and she felt her heart start to beat at double speed as she realised what he had just said.

'That's exactly like me!' Linnet cried wildly. 'I have those markings too. Why are you telling me this? What's it all got to do with me?' She thumped the badger's hairy flank hard and burst into a storm of sobbing. She was horribly frightened, and yet she now felt a compulsion to listen to the end. 'Go on,' she gulped, smearing tears and snot over her face with badger-smelling hands. 'I-I'd b-b-better know the worst.'

'As Rhiannon finished speaking,' the badger continued, 'a girl stepped forward. She was thirteen years old with deep red hair, one cornflower blue eye and one emerald green one. She had a streak of silver hair behind her right ear, and as she knelt before Rhiannon she drew it back to show a birthmark, shaped like a clover leaf.

'"I am the Maiden you seek," she said. "I will tame the worldwyrm and lead him back to his long sleep. But my Power is not great and I do not know the way."

Linnet clutched at the badger, as the meaning of Sunstar's words sank in. The double beat of her heart changed to a cold, bone-deep fear pouring into her veins and freezing them solid with realisation. 'I am this Maiden, aren't I?' she panted. 'Those dreams I had last night and those visions I've been having all day . . . that wyrm is here again and you want *me* to send it back, don't you? But I can't! I don't know how, just like that other girl.' She began to cry softly again and Sunstar nuzzled her with his whiskery muzzle.

'Hush, child, hush! The story is not ended yet. Listen on and do not despair. You will see that you are not alone in this.' Linnet quietened, her breathing quick in the still air of the cavern. Then she erupted again.

'But I *really* can't,' she gasped defiantly. 'I won't! I'm not a wyccan. The only magic I know involves my father's *beer* – and even that's just a silly kind of technomagic, not *old* magic like this! I don't know about wyrms! I don't know *anything*, n-n-not even Frankish verbs! I don't care how many people there are to help, I still *don't-know-how*!'

'Then let me tell you,' said the badger crossly. 'And don't interrupt again, because time is getting short. The first Maiden was helped by the strongest of old magics to send the wyrm back into the deepest core of earth. It was bound there in sleep with a dragonwort elixir provided by a sorceress of the Fey Folk, and the Maiden was given much honour and released from her task for that time. It was then that the Six Guardians were chosen to watch over it. The humans and the beast changed as they needed to – and I am only the latest in a long line of badger Guardians – but the magical beings have been there from the beginning.

'Over the centuries the wyrm became restless, and it tossed and turned round the earth's heart until its head came near the surface again in this place that is now called Wyrmesbury. It has always been a spot where the magical currents of this world are at their strongest, because the Door to Avvallon lies under Hootcat Hill.

'Mankind took the Fire that the wyrm had spewed forth in his rampaging and used it to their own advantage. So eventually the Six went into hiding where they had been able to work openly before, and they waited and secretly watched the place in Wyrmesbury where the wyrm's head lay.

'The Fey Queen too was bound by the old magic to do her part, since she had interfered at the beginning. She and one half of the Fey people were sentenced to guard the wyrm at all times, changing over with the Fey Prince and the other half of the Fey every seven years. They were forced to adapt their forms in order to survive in the mortal world, and to dance in Black Meadows if the wyrm stirred in its bed – which it often did. That's why Wyrmesbury has so many earthquakes, and why the Meadows have the reputation for being haunted.

'Added to that the oldest of the Fey, a tricksy, cunning sorceress called Fidget Reedglitter was bound by magic to make the dragonwort elixir and keep it and the magical Chalice of Athyr ready in case the wyrm woke. But now Fidget Reedglitter uses the dragonwort elixir for her Queen's benefit – to keep her eternally young and beautiful. She still keeps it and the Chalice of Athyr, but no living being now knows where they are except her. It will be your first and most important task as Maiden to find them.' He went on, as Linnet gaped at him, speechless for once as she tried to take in what he had said so casually.

'As well as saying Black Meadows were haunted, rumours also sprang up – spread by outsiders – saying that treasure was buried there, and once in a while a greedy man from Vesterton or elsewhere would brave the rumour and dig, despite our wards, for greed is a Power greater than any magic, and then the wyrm would be disturbed and rise again, and wreak havoc in its anger.

'It last happened nearly five hundred years ago, in my great-great grandfather's grandfather's day, and the wyrm was subdued again then with great difficulty. The reborn Maiden had to be summoned into her Power once more. Now Tom Bickerspike has woken the wyrm again with his meddling technomachine. As you saw in your dream, he has paid the price for his greed.' He stopped, watching Linnet carefully. She now felt a huge anger welling up inside her. She didn't want any of this. Everyday life was difficult enough. Why couldn't her life be *normal* like other people's? Why couldn't this Maiden be someone else?

'Why?' she yelled, sending Skystone and the blue kobold into a flutter of startlement. 'Tell me why I shouldn't run back to the real world where there isn't any of this old magic or wyrms or Maidens . . . or any of this really scary stuff about outwitting a mad Fey sorceress. Why shouldn't I just leave right now and let this wyrm do what it wants?' She stood there in a blind fury, deaf to anything but her own fear and panic.

Sunstar suddenly reared up onto his hind legs and put his paws on Linnet's shoulders, weighing her down until her feet felt welded to the earth. His warm badgery breath flowed over her face like a soothing spell, calming her mutinous thoughts and words until she could hear him again.

'Linnet Perry, you are the only one who can do this. The worldwyrm could rise again at any time, and then no one will be safe.'

Linnet looked straight into the badger's black eyes, her fury all drained away for the time being. She felt suddenly very tired.

'I still don't understand,' she said wearily. 'How did this all happen to *me*? And who are these Guardians who are supposed to help me, anyway?' Sunstar sighed. This modern habit of asking questions was not something he'd been trained to deal with. Previous Maidens had been . . . more amenable, he thought.

'There is so much to tell in such a short time, and we must be up at the Owlstones on Hootcat Hill before moonrise. But I will do my best to answer you. The Five other Guardians you will meet later. Three of them – the human ones – you know already, though you will perhaps be very surprised indeed at who they must be in their daily lives in Wyrmesbury. Then there is me. Badgers have been Guardians from the first – we are patient and long-lived, and we remember things. Rhiannon has been a Guardian since the time of the first Maiden, and she is very Powerful still in the old magics, though we are all less than we were. Last is Cernunnos, the Stagman who lives among the rocks on Cerne Tump. He is wild, and dangerous, but he is the protector of Beasts and untamed things, and he walks as easily in Avvallon as on the earth. All of us are sworn to help and serve the Maiden in her task, if it should come in our time of Guardianship.

'As for why you are the Maiden – the way of choosing is a secret of the old magic, which has long been lost to us. The Perry blood is ancient, and you are descended through your father from those humans with wyzard magic I told you about. One of them was Tam Lynn the Rhymer, the only mortal musician to escape the Fey Queen. Your name echoes his, and perhaps that link is in itself the reason. Whatever the explanation, you *are* the Maiden. I woke at your first cry, and no Badger has ever been wrong about that.'

'But why can't we just blow the wyrm up with a technobomb or something?' asked Linnet, feeling recalcitrant again. 'Why do we need it anyway?' The badger sighed again. He'd known Linnet was stubborn, but why couldn't she just accept things as they were?

'As for blowing up the worldwyrm, it is made by the oldest magic of all – the same magic that made the earth. It is both our curse and our blessing, for we cannot do without it. The weight of the wyrm protects the earth's heart and balances the earth as it turns around the sun, and if it were not there at the centre of things, we should simply spiral off into space. Now, child, there is no time for more talking. We must go, for the earth magic will run strongest until midnight tomorrow. Come to the Owlstones, Linnet Perry, and then we shall see what to do.'

Linnet followed Sunstar silently, the bluewinged Kobold following behind her. Frankish verbs seemed as far away as the full moon just rising over Hootcat Hill, and the burning desire to ask questions had left her – for the moment.

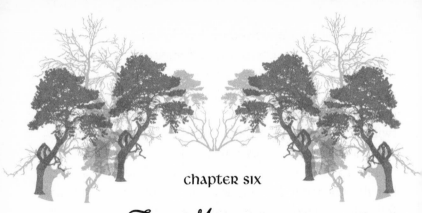

chapter six

The Meeting on
Hootcat Hill

Six Gifts for the Maiden,
At Beltain's deepest hour
Six Gifts for the Maiden
To bring her to her Power...

from 'The Prophecies of the Seven'

The Owlstones peered out through the heavy mist
that surrounded them, their carven bird faces
impassive under the lichen and mosses that covered them.
Professor Tyto Hullart stood among them, watching, as
the last rays of sunlight faded behind the trees, turning
the leaves golden. He drew the hood of his long brown
cloak – the muted colour of hootcat feathers – over his
bald head, and walked over to the nearest, reaching out
to touch its carving with a long finger as he whispered a
word of Power. The stone shivered at his touch, and the
carving opened its beak and let out a low, creaking hoot.

'Come, my hootcat brothers,' said the Professor. 'It is time to wake.' The carving spread silent wings and flew to his shoulder, blending perfectly into the cloak. Five minutes later, each of the nine stones but one had a hootcat perched on it, golden eyes searching the growing twilight as they sat, hooting softly. The stones themselves were now bare of any carving at all.

The roar of a powerful motorbike at the foot of the hill drowned out the hooting for a moment, and then fell silent. Two figures, one very large, the other considerably shorter and rather plump, came up Hootcat Hill towards the trees. Each made a quick twisting sign as they reached the mist that surrounded the Owlstones, and it parted in front of them and then closed as they came through.

Fay Morgan wore a green cloak, and she carried a silver cauldron under one arm. Wayland Smith was dressed in bright red biking leathers, embroidered with silver sledgehammers. He bore a small anvil, and there were tools slung carelessly on the broad belt around his broad waist.

'As fine a Beltain Evening as I ever saw,' he growled. 'Where is everybody?'

'The moon is not yet rising,' said Professor Hullart. 'They will be here soon enough.' As he spoke, something silvery flowed down from Rinnon's Crest and moved towards them. Eyes without Power would not have seen it at all as it glided past Maiden's Mount and vanished. Moments later there was a shimmering in the glade, and Rhiannon appeared, her three birds fluttering round her head.

'Greetings, Lady,' said Professor Hullart, bowing low. 'It has been long and long since we saw you here.'

'Greetings, Owlman,' said Rhiannon. 'And greetings to you too, Wyccan and Smith. It *has* been long and long.' There was a crashing in the trees and a great stag bounded into the clearing. It was the Stagman, Cernunnos.

'Now we are Five,' said Rhiannon, 'and the moon is about to rise. It is time.' As she spoke, a blue light appeared across the fields, moving fast. 'The Maiden is coming. Let us make ready while I tell you of the news I have received from the underdwellers, and from Avvallon.'

Linnet stumbled and panted through the green hayfield after Sunstar. Her socks and trainers were soaked and heavy with dew and seeds, and her mind still felt numb and slow with the weight of all she had just learned. The Blue Kobold whirred and flew about her, urging her on with their shrill voices. Hootcat Hill lay before her in the gathering darkness, its top an immense shadowy blackness, shrouded in white mist. She found that for the very first time she could look at it directly without her eyes wanting to slide away. Above it an unearthly light started to glow silvery golden on the tree tops – the full moon was rising. Sunstar stopped and turned to face her.

'Do not be afraid,' he said. 'You were born to this, whether you believe it yet or not. You are strong in Power, Linnet Perry, maybe stronger than any Maiden that has ever lived because you have a dual heritage. You are the first Maiden in whom old magic and the new technomagic is mixed. Here, tonight, you will learn something of what that Power means.' The full moon glow was fiercer now, laying a path of rays from the summit to the foot. Linnet felt another small surge of rebellion rise up inside her, but it was too late, the Blue Kobold were hurrying her forward to stand beside the Badger, a guard of honour in miniature.

'Come, Maiden,' he said. 'Walk the moonpath with me.'

As Linnet stepped onto that path of unearthly light she felt a tingling in her feet, which quickly rose throughout her whole body. Words chased through her head, powerful words she had never heard before, but instantly knew the meaning of. Hootcat owls cried out above her head.

The Blue Kobold flitted away to stand guard outside the stones. Then Linnet the Maiden and Sunstar the Badger came to the top of Hootcat Hill in the light of a Beltain full moon, and stepped through the mists and in between the Owlstones to the centre of the circle, where five Guardians were waiting for them.

Linnet gasped as she recognised three of the five figures before her.

'Professor Hullart ... and ... and Miss Morgan ... and *you*!' She whirled and looked at the large figure of Wayland Smith. 'But you're Dad's best friend! You came to supper on Wednesday and mended Dad's spade! And I borrowed a book from the library on Friday. And I bought toothpaste the same day. Why didn't any of you ever *tell* me about all this?' she wailed, all feelings of

Power leaving her in a rush.

'Because they were sworn not to, Linnet Perry,' said a deep, whinnying voice. 'They have known your potential to be the Maiden since the hour you were born, and have guarded you all your short life. If the worldwyrm had not been awoken, you would have gone about your life as an ordinary girl living in an extraordinary place. You would never have met any of us in this guise.

'But come, now it is time for you to take your place as the Seventh Guardian. Each of us has something for you.' She stepped forward and held out a tiny silver horseshoe, hung on a chain that shimmered like moonshine. Then her voice changed, and the sound of thundering hooves was in it.

'I am Rhiannon, Daughter of Mares. Will you accept my Gift and your place as Maiden?'

The Owlstones stood, waiting silently, poised for Linnet's decision. She felt suddenly rudderless, adrift in a strange sea with no familiar landmarks to steer by. Then she saw Wayland Smith's familiar figure looming to her left. Surely if her father's best friend was here it would be all right? But what if it wasn't? What if she couldn't do it? Linnet took a deep, calming breath and closed her eyes, trying to think, to decide. At once, she felt the strange tingling rise up from her feet again. She felt a door in her mind snap open – one which had been shut all her life till now. Voices drifted out of it – voices that she knew instinctively were those of all the Maidens who had ever been.

'We will help you,' they said. 'We are your Maiden memories and we will guide you. Take up your Power.'

'Do I have to?' she said to the voices inside her head, wondering as she did so if perhaps she was going a bit mad – whether she was talking to no one except herself. 'Because all this is really scary.'

'Do not be afraid. We are here. We are you, and you are us. Take up your rightful place in the world. We know you can do it. You are the strongest of us all.'

Linnet drew another breath and smiled wryly at the long line of Maidens she could now see peering out of that door in her mind. They all had red hair. They looked friendly. Like sisters. 'Thank you. That helps. A bit. I think,' she said to them silently. Then she opened her eyes, and saw the Being standing before her, tall, cloaked in gold and garlanded with moondaisies. She stared deep into Rhiannon's large, horselike eyes. 'Thank you,' she said again, this time out loud. 'I will . . .' She stopped and clenched her fists for courage. 'I will accept your Gift,' she said in a rush. There. She had done it. There was a sound of clapping in her mind. Rhiannon stepped forward and placed the chain round her neck. It felt as cold as clouds, as light as moonshine.

At that moment the world shifted slightly and settled in a new place – a place with a Maiden in it.

'Call on this if you need speed, and I will send help,' Rhiannon said. Then she took Linnet's hand and led her clockwise round the circle to where Fay Morgan stood by her cauldron.

'In this place, Linnet, I am the Wyccan, the weaver of air. Will you accept my Gift and your place as Maiden?'

And she leaned over her cauldron and breathed on it. Streams of brightly coloured air swirled up and into the crystal bottle she held ready.

'I will accept your Gift,' said Linnet, though she was finding it entirely bizarre to admit that a person she had known all her life could change from an ordinary chymist in a white lab coat to this mysterious cloaked figure in green. The bottle felt both cold and hot in her hand as she put it in her pocket.

'Blue for sleep, green for concealment, red for earth Power, yellow for healing, purple for mindspeaking, white for skyforce. I will teach you how to call them out later. Come to me tomorrow evening,' Fay whispered.

Next, Rhiannon led her round the circle to where Cernunnos stood.

'Welcome, Maiden,' he said, and even his quietest tones roared and belled round the stones like a rutting autumn stag. 'I am the Stagman, Cernunnos. Will you accept my Gift and your place as Maiden?' He held out a cloak of softest white doeskin, embroidered with a winding pattern of silver clover flowers that led the eye astray.

Linnet glanced up at him through her eyelashes as she went through the acceptance ritual once more. Cernunnos was in man form now, but still his horns swayed and stood out against the moon like great tree branches. He was the most frightening thing she'd ever seen, totally wild and alien, with a scent of ancient moss and forests coming from the green leaves that covered his face and body. Only his eyes shone out, brown, with small orange flames within.

'This cloak will give you courage as well as hiding you from unfriendly eyes if you are chased. Put it on, Maiden.'

And it was true, as Linnet put the cloak on, she felt a bit braver than she had all evening. She looked the Stagman properly in the eyes then.

'Thank you, Cernunnos,' she said gravely. 'But I think that really I will have to deal with the deepest dreads myself, like I always do. No cloak is going to take those away.'

Cernunnos laughed. 'See, you have the courage to stand up to me already!'

Rhiannon led her to Professor Hullart, who had been her guide and helper through the stormy seas of literature from the moment she first discovered her difficulties with reading. She gazed at him, noticing his strange eyes for the first time as if a veil had been lifted from her own.

'For you, Linnet, I have this,' he said, as she stood before him. 'Here I am the Owlman, and this circle is my place. Do you accept my Gift and your place as Maiden?'

Linnet nodded once more, and he plucked a pale hootcat feather from his cloak, brushing it lightly over her eyes, nose, lips and ears.

'Now you have the Power of speech and summoning with all living creatures, not just Sunstar.' As he spoke, the hootcat on his shoulder and the eight on the stones all hooted.

'Greetings, Maiden,' they said. Linnet's eyes opened very wide.

'Greetings, hootcats,' she stammered, but anyone

outside that circle who had been listening would have heard only another owl.

Rhiannon took her round to Sunstar. 'Badgers are known for never letting go,' he said. 'Will you accept my Gift of strength and your place as Maiden?'

'Yes, Sunstar,' said Linnet. 'I will.'

Sunstar coughed once or twice and then breathed over her as he had done in the mound. This time a golden mist rose up around Linnet's body, and sank into her skin, leaving faint sparkles behind as it did so. She felt it settle deep into her very centre.

'Remember, strength is not just of the body,' he said.

Linnet looked up at Wayland Smith. Gone was the oily, begrimed best friend of her father, who let her blow his forge bellows, and sit on his motorbike. But he was still utterly familiar and comforting for all that, and as she looked he winked at her broadly. She grinned back, gesturing at his red embroidered bike leathers. 'Nice suit.' Wayland Smith bowed mockingly in wordless thanks. Then his face turned more serious, and he spoke.

'Linnet. In this place I am the Smith, as I always am and always have been. Will you accept my Gift and your place as Maiden?'

'Thank you, Wayland. I will,' she said. Then Wayland Smith set his anvil down and took a long, delicate hammer from his belt.

'Fire,' he commanded. And a cold, blue fire sprang up around him. Working quickly, he took a small lump of silver from his pocket, and turned and twisted and hammered it until it began to take shape as a small pouch with a flap and a silver tassel in the shape of a cloverleaf to fasten it. With a final flourish he gave it one last tap. 'Dowse,' he said. And the fire disappeared. 'This pouch is made of living silver, the only existing piece of it left,' he said. 'It will take whatever you put in it, either big or small, and never let it be lost or stolen or broken.' Linnet threaded it onto her own belt, and put the Wyccan's Gift inside it. It was as soft and pliable as leather.

'Now you have been Gifted by all of us,' said Rhiannon. 'But what of your Gift to yourself, Maiden?'

'Er – what Gift?' asked Linnet, surprised. 'I – I don't have a Gift to give myself. Do I?' she finished uncertainly.

'Of course you do,' said Fay Morgan. 'What do you think your own Power is, if not a Gift to yourself?'

'Oh,' said Linnet, feeling even more unsure now, and dropping her head forward so that her hair hid her face, which she was sure was turning red. In spite of all the wonderful things she'd just been given, she still couldn't really believe that she had any real Power of her own. 'Um. What do I have to do? It seems really weird giving myself a Gift – kind of embarrassing.' Wayland laughed.

'Linnet, Linnet! It's time to stop hiding behind that flaming hair of yours. Can you think of nothing at all you'd like to give yourself? Not even a little thing?'

Linnet looked up at him and tossed her hair back crossly. He was always laughing at her, and she never had a clever answer for him – at least she hadn't until now. She felt the doeskin of Cernunnos's cloak under her fingers, and Sunstar's golden breath coiling inside her, making her brave.

'Yes,' she shot back at him. 'I'd like to see you laugh on

the other side of that hairy face of yours!' She didn't wait for a reaction, turning instead to Rhiannon. 'What do I have to do to give myself this Gift?' she asked. Rhiannon put both hands on Linnet's shoulders.

'You must step into the Power that has been waiting for you all these long years and accept it within yourself absolutely. For only then will you truly be a part of the Circle of Guardians.'

'But what if I don't want to?' Linnet asked, wanting to let out a last burst of rebellion, though she knew it was futile. She had already committed herself to this path when she listened to her Maiden memories and accepted her first Gift. Rhiannon sighed and stamped impatiently, her foot almost sounding like a hoof thumping on the soft grass.

'Then you will not be able to fulfil your task. The worldwyrm will rage unchecked, and the heart of our world will be destroyed, unbalanced and sent whirling into the sun to die.' Linnet set her hands on her hips and stared defiantly round the circle. There is definitely no way out, she thought. I'll have to give myself this scary Power thing and learn to cope with it, like I cope with everything else in my life. Probably badly, she thought, knowing my luck so far.

'I do accept my own Power absolutely as my Gift to myself.' The words came out before she could stop them and she felt the world shift again and turn in a new way. She had said it, and the decision was over. She looked round the circle and felt a huge sense of relief that she now had another kind of family to help her through this. But it was all going so fast, and she had to slow it down, make it hers somehow. 'Now, tell me how I step into it or whatever it is I have to do?'

Fay laughed as Rhiannon took a step backwards in dismay at Linnet's almost flippant tone. 'You've never met a modern teenager, have you, Lady?'

'No,' snorted Rhiannon. 'I can see that Maidens are not as meek as they once were. Child, this is not a game. Your Power must be accepted from your heart, not just your mouth.' Linnet looked at her and sighed inwardly. Time for putting on her best mollify-Mum mode.

'I truly do accept it,' she said. 'I felt the change as soon as I said the words. But it's all been very sudden and a lot to take in. You've always been like this – I only learned properly what I was just now, and it's big and frightening and . . . and I still feel like someone who has Physicks homework, not like someone who can talk to animals, and defeat dragons. Anyway I really *don't* know how to step into my Power unless you show me, or what to do afterwards with this wyrm.' She fell silent. It was all too true. I'm going to be completely useless at this, she thought, and I wish it would all lighten up a bit.

'So let us all join hands and paws, let the Circle of Guardians be completed, and then you will know,' Rhiannon said softly. They all moved to the centre of the Owlstones, Linnet between Rhiannon and Sunstar, a hand that felt somehow like a hoof on her left, and a solid furry paw on her right.

Then, from nowhere, the chanting started, as the old magic began to take shape within her, and she suddenly knew she wasn't going to be useless after all.

'Whatever happens, do not let go,' said Sunstar, softly, as he joined in the spell.

> *Is mall gach cos air chassan agn eolus*
> *On unknown paths all feet are slow*
> *Chan eil tuil air nach tig traoghadh*
> *Every flood must ebb and go*
> *Ni heolas go haontios*
> *Power as One in Seven hands*
> *Is binn gach eun 'na dhoire fhein*
> *Sweet sings the bird in her own lands*

The spell gripped her in its jaws and consumed her. All at the same time, Linnet felt as if the earth was swallowing her and squeezing her whole body tighter than her father's biggest bearhug. She was flying in a dark sky full of stars, drowning in a deep green sea and breathing, she was the burning hub of a volcano, the iceberg's rainbow core. Time slowed and slithered until in the centuries-long moments between one excruciating heart's beat and the next she slipped through the open door in her mind and held out her hands to a long line of red-headed girls just like herself. As she Gifted herself with the Maiden's Power, she became their minds, and they became hers – a myriad Maidens, yet only one all-encompassing Maiden memory.

Then the spell twisted – altered – took her to another plane of being. Linnet felt the shattering pain of knowing each stone, each leaf, each bird and animal and insect in the world around her, their living and their dying. For one terrible, wonderful, awesome moment she shattered into a million, billion uncountable Linnets and became at one and the same time *everything* and *everywhere*, and understood them utterly. And then it all stopped, and she found herself in a different place. The Circle of Seven was still complete, but they were now standing in a hilltop meadow of cowslips and daisies, with a pool at its centre. The Owlstones were nowhere to be seen and the full moon was high in the sky above.

'*Is binn gach eun 'na dhoire fhein,*' she whispered. '*Sweet sings the bird in her own lands*. This is Maiden's Mount, my own place of Power. I feel . . . different here.' She felt her face with steady fingers. 'Am I still Linnet Perry?'

'Look in the pool, Linnet,' said Fay's soft voice. 'Then you will see.' So Linnet looked and was relieved to see that her face at least had not changed. As for the Power that now filled her, she knew that it would transform her forever. There was no going back. Now she was truly one of the Seven.

'*On unknown paths all feet are slow,*' she said. 'And mine will be at first. But I won't fail you. At least, I'll try not to.'

'And we will help as we can,' said Rhiannon. 'You know how to call each of us now, as well as others who may help you. There is much for you to learn from some of us before you are ready to confront the worldwyrm. Your Power is still new and untried.'

It was suddenly all too much – too serious. Humour was definitely needed here. Linnet rolled her eyes and grinned. 'No exams, right? Please tell me no exams.'

'What are *exams*?' asked Rhiannon and Cernunnos, bewildered.

'Never mind!' sighed the three human Guardians in unison.

chapter seven

Lessons in Power

Is fusa tuitim na eirigh—
Falling is easier than rising.

from 'Proverbs of Old MacDubh'

'*L*innet, *Linnet!*' called her mother. 'Breakfast! Now!' Linnet rolled out of bed and hit the floor groaning. How could she go to school after last night? How could she concentrate on stupid bauxite mines and the right spellings for an English essay on Shakspear with all the Power rioting and roiling round in her head – not to mention several whole new sets of memories? It just wasn't possible. She heard footsteps on the stairs and her door banged open.

'Linnet! What is the *matter* with you?' asked Nyneve Perry. 'Are you ill or something? Look at you, you're not even dressed!' She came over and laid a cool hand against Linnet's forehead. 'No, no temperature.' Linnet brushed her away impatiently. Trust Mum to show an interest in her just when it wasn't wanted.

'I'm just *tired*, OK, Mum? Sorry if it's a crime. I studied late and then I couldn't sleep. You know how hard I find reading things.' Well, that wasn't too much of a lie, she thought.

'Hurry up then, or you'll miss the bus. You'll have to eat your toast on the way.'

Linnet tossed her half-eaten burnt toast into a hedge and ran down the hill, her heavy bag banging on her back. She had far too much going on in her brain to concentrate on eating, and anyway, after Professor Hullart's Gift of language, she was totally entranced and distracted by the novelty of understanding the morning voices of the birds singing about worms and nests and eggs, not to mention the tiny voices of the insects.

'Oi, watch out, bigfeet,' yelled a large stagbeetle crossing the path in front of her. She had just leapt over him, frantically avoiding a messy accident when she heard a shout.

'Wait! Linnet!' called a familiar voice behind her. Oh no! Petroc. What on earth was she going to tell him? Well, none of the Guardians had told her she couldn't confide in her best friend. And even if they had . . . she clutched her head and groaned again. This was definitely not going to be a good day. What if he didn't believe her?

Petroc rushed up, dark tight-curled hair flopping over his eyes, and his burly six foot frame untucked and untidy as usual. 'Hey, Linn, did you hear about the thing at the Bickerspike's? Really bizarre stuff. What do you think happened?' He stopped and looked at her face, whiter than usual, but with a sense of glowing Power that hadn't been there when he had last seen her the previous Friday. 'Er, is something else going on, Linn?' he enquired nervously.

Fifteen minutes later, after a whispered conversation on the bus, Petroc sat back and stared at Linnet. His mouth was slightly open, his brown eyes were round and a bit wild at the edges, and his usually dark skin had gone the colour of milky coffee. Linnet had been telling him for years about the strange colours she saw round people – she said he was bright green – and her differentness was one of the things he liked about her. But this stuff about a dragonwyrm thing eating Young Tom (who he rather resented, because he knew Linnet fancied him, even though he knew it was a bit dog in the manger, since he didn't fancy her himself) was beyond weird, and as for this Maiden stuff – well, that was just plain crazy.

'I know we both have to live in the mad world of Wyrmesbury, but are you *sure* it wasn't just another one of your dreams, Linn?'

'I knew you wouldn't believe me,' hissed Linnet. 'Look at when I dreamed your sister's cello disappeared and reappeared in the middle of Gold Street. And it did. My dreams happen to be true, in case you hadn't noticed. And as of two nights ago that isn't a *good* thing.' She thought hard for a while, hatching a plan. It meant abusing the Gift Professor Hullart had given her, but right now she didn't really care about that. Convincing her best friend was more important than anything. 'Just watch what happens when They try it on today. Then you'll see.' Her Maiden memories twittered warnings in the back of her head. But she made a determined effort and shut them out. She wasn't surprised at how easy it was – she'd been shutting stuff out all her life.

'OK. But I'll be right behind you, just in case whatever you're planning doesn't work,' said Petroc, carefully keeping a straight face. His best mate some kind of important magical person? Surely she must have gone even more out of her mind than usual? And as for Miss Morgan being some kind of witch – she was his auntie's best friend. He would have heard *something* – wouldn't he?

Linnet punched him on the shoulder. Hard. She knew exactly what he was thinking.

'Just watch me,' she hissed fiercely.

'Calm down, Linn, I will,' he said. There was a sparking, fizzing, hot feeling in the air around his friend, and the generations of strange Wyrmesbury blood he usually tried not to think about told him urgently that this was going to get ugly.

Tony Skink was the first of Them to see Linnet. He bent and pulled a wad of dried and crusted gum off his shoe and hurled it at her. It hit her hard on the nose as Tony ran off, laughing.

'Right,' said Linnet. 'That's it.' She walked the way Tony had gone, forming the image of bees in her head as she went. Lots of bees. A loud buzzing began to fill the air around her. It was coming from her mouth.

'What are you *doing*,' panted Petroc behind her.

'Summoning,' said Linnet calmly around the bee noise, although inside she was fizzing with excitement and terror at what she was planning to do next. 'Just summoning.'

The rest of Them were lounging on the playground wall by the Chymistry block, scribbling rude graffiti and laughing. Everyone else was giving them a wide berth. As Linnet walked around the corner with Petroc close behind, a silence fell.

'Get her!' yelled Lellicia Sundew. 'I've got bruises I want paid for.' But as They started for Linnet, bags swinging and fists forward, Linnet said a word of Power and threw up a magical barrier of invisible thistles just in front of her. They slammed into it and rocked back, cursing and whimpering and picking prickles out of Themselves. Then, as one, They screamed in fear as a huge swarm of bees erupted out of a hole in the air and began stinging Them. They scattered and ran. Linnet clutched her head suddenly as thousands of dying bee voices sounded within her head, each a tiny blossom of pain.

'No,' she said. 'NO! You weren't meant to die . . .'

Then she lost control of her Power completely in her panic, and the bees began to sting everyone. She felt a hand shaking her arm.

'Linn, Linn! You have to stop them. Now! Call them off – unsummon them or whatever you have to do. I . . . I think someone's badly hurt.'

Linnet found a tiny hole in the Power and summoned the remaining bees through it, sobbing with effort. Every small insect death stabbed her soul until she was staggering under the weight of them.

Petroc shook her again. 'Snap out of it,' he said urgently. 'You have to do something.'

She looked up. People were tearing around the play-ground, rubbing their stings and screaming. But in one corner, someone was on the ground, writhing. It was Tony Skink. His black skin had turned ashy brown-grey and he was blue round the lips and wheezing for breath. Linnet began to run towards the classrooms to get help.

'Whoa!' said a voice, as she crashed into a large man. 'What's going on, Linnet Perry.' It was the headmaster, Mr Pikestaff.

'Bees,' she gasped. 'Tony . . . stung . . . allergic, I think . . . get a Medipod . . .' Then she stepped into the shadows and began to draw the Power back in, undoing the spell until not a trace of it remained. It was much harder than releasing it. Her teeth were chattering with fear and shock, and her Maiden memories had escaped her grip and were scolding inside her head. She let them. She deserved it.

Minutes later, a silver Medipod was hovering over the playground and Tony was surrounded by white figures inserting needles into him. The school nurse was handing out dollops of soothing gel to everyone else who had been stung.

Mr Pikestaff walked into the centre of the playground and clapped his hands. 'Right. Everyone back to class when you've been attended to. Tony's going to be fine. Excitement's over.' There was not a bee to be seen. Even the small dead bodies had disappeared. He peered around and muttered to himself, 'Extraordinary. Where did they all go. I'd better call the Pest Officer to investigate.'

Linnet walked towards the Geography classroom. Petroc came up beside her. 'It all went a bit wrong,' she said.

'Yeah,' he said. 'It did. And I reckon what you had your little magic bees do to Them just now makes you as bad as They are, not to mention everyone else getting hurt, and Tony nearly dying.'

Linnet whirled round. She already felt guilty enough, and now even her best friend was on her case. 'What?' she shouted. 'They bully me ever since I came here, and you complain when they get a taste of their own medicine? They were just meant to get stung a bit. I didn't know Tony was allergic . . . I didn't mean for anyone else but Them to get hurt . . . I didn't mean for the bees to die.' Her voice had dropped to a whisper.

Petroc looked at her, his face hard. He felt angry and scared and like he didn't know his best friend properly any more. And he'd *felt* her do her bee magic – like something inside him had just woken up and recognised her Power for what it was. That was scariest of all.

'I know you didn't know about Tony, but yeah, I do complain. You didn't stand up to them yourself. You hid behind something else, just like you always do. Except this time it wasn't me doing my usual menacing impression of a strongman that doesn't work half the time anyway. It was real Power that brought those bees in. I felt it. It was horrible. And if you use magic every time you get into trouble with ordinary people you'll just turn into some sort of mad tyrant person – who won't even take responsibility for sorting out their own life. You'd better do something about that before you even start on dealing with this wyrm thing. Because I reckon you'll be on your own when you face it. There won't be anyone to hide behind then.'

He turned and stomped into the Geography classroom, slamming the door behind him angrily. Linnet took a shaky breath and burst into tears. Then the bell rang, and a rush of other pupils pushed past her. Wiping her eyes, she followed Petroc into class.

Petroc wouldn't speak to her at morning break, and she stood on her own, looking at Them huddled in a corner, plasters all over them, watching her with edgy, unforgiving eyes. Maybe Petroc was right. She shut her own eyes and felt the Power stirring lazily within her. She had a deep instinctive knowing that it was meant to be used for good, and yet the first thing she had done with Professor Hullart's Gift was to hurt other people — ordinary humans, who, however horrible to her personally, were the ones she was meant to be saving from the wyrm's devastation. She had nearly killed one of Them. Did that really make her worse than Them? She was very much afraid it did. Linnet opened her eyes and marched over to Lellicia Sundew, who cringed back from her. Time to take Petroc's advice.

'You've got no right to go around terrorising anyone who's a bit different to you, but what happened this morning wasn't right either. I should have told you years ago just to sod off and leave me alone. I'm telling you now.' She said it in a rush, and even to herself, her voice sounded weak and shaky.

'Wouldn't have made a difference,' sneered Lellicia. 'You're weird, and weird people deserve all they get.'

'No, they don't,' snapped Linnet, suddenly furious. 'Everyone deserves respect. Including me. And I'm not weird. I'm quite nice, if you'd ever bothered to try and find that out.'

'Yeah, right. You've got some kind of creepy invisible wall stuff going on that stops people going near you, you call freaky killer bees out of nowhere, and you're trying to pretend you're just like us. Maybe you might have been what you call "normal" last week, but you're definitely not now. Just keep away from us, weirdo.' And to that Linnet had no reply, because it was mostly true. She turned away and walked over to Petroc.

'I tried,' she said. 'I did try.'

'I saw.'

Later that evening she walked down Wychbold Street and knocked on the door of the chymist's shop. Her parents were out again, but she had told them she was studying with Petroc, in case she was late. Petroc had grudgingly agreed to lie for her, if asked. His mother was still with his grandmother, who was very ill, and his dad was away working in the big City, so only his elder sister, Zafira, was at home just now, and as usual when she wasn't studying for her degree at music college she spent all her time in her room listening to classical music and playing her 'cello.

'You'd better learn to use this Power thing,' he said sourly. 'Or you might decide to set something on me next. I get enough bruises from cricket balls.' He still hadn't properly forgiven her, but he had shared his chocolate bar with her on the bus, so she hoped he might by the morning. Petroc wasn't one to hold grudges, but she had definitely scared him. And that was something else she was going to have to deal with, because she didn't want to be someone who scared their best friend.

Fay Morgan answered the knock at once, and took her through to the back of the shop. Linnet was relieved to see she looked quite normal again in her usual clothes, but the relief disappeared as soon as she saw what was waiting for her in the room behind the curtain. The huge silver-grey cat sat upright in the chair and looked at her out of large, green eyes.

'Good evening, Linnet,' he purred.

'This,' said Fay, 'is Arculus Havnor.'

'How do you do?' Linnet asked politely. Arculus Havnor was definitely a cat who warranted politeness, she thought. His paws were each the size of a small milk saucer, and his tail was thicker than Linnet's wrist. She had not yet seen his claws or teeth, and she thought perhaps that she didn't want to.

'Have you brought the Gift I gave you?' asked Fay. Linnet reached into Wayland Smith's pouch and pulled it out. 'Do you remember what the colours are for?'

'Blue for sleep, green for concealment, red for earth Power, yellow for healing, purple for mindspeaking, white for skyforce,' Linnet recited parrot fashion. 'But what does all that mean, exactly? I sort of understand, but how does it work?'

'That,' said Fay, 'is what Arculus and I are going to show you.' She took the bottle and set it in the middle of the table. 'Stand beside me, Linnet. Now, Arculus, the shield, please.' Arculus Havnor's purr became even louder, and out of his mouth poured a dense silver-grey light that whirled upwards, above and around them. The note changed suddenly, and the light became a transparent, swaying dome that enclosed them totally.

'What is it?' asked Linnet nervously.

'Protection,' said Fay. 'Nothing can get in, or out, so you're completely safe even if you make a mistake. Arculus is very good at it.' The cat looked smug, the tip of his tail twitching slightly. Then he lay down in the chair and seemingly went to sleep.

'Do you remember the wind wisdom you learnt last night?' Linnet closed her eyes, and immediately the songs of the wind rose in her mind, all the winds of the world from the easterly helm wind of the Pennines and the squally brubru of the Indies to the autumnal papagayo of Brazil and the sand-laden simoom of the Arabian desert. Every wind told her a story of rising and falling, of air and sky and the shapes of blown things.

'I remember,' she said.

'Then I shall first teach you the spell called "wind seeking the harbours".' Fay took the bottle and shook it. The myriad colours swirled and spun. 'These were tuned to me, but now you must learn to make them obey you. Take the bottle and open it, and say the spell . . .

> *'A ghaoth ag iarraidh na'm port,*
> *Come safe to harbour and haven, O wind.'*

Linnet did as she was told, briefly amazed at how the strange words tumbled off her tongue with no slips or hesitations. The strands of air immediately formed themselves into a column in front of her, twining and intertwining in an endless dance.

'Now call the one you need for concealment,' instructed

Fay softly. 'It's the easiest.' Linnet pulled with her mind at the green strand. At once it wrapped itself around her, although she felt nothing as it touched her. She looked down at her toes. They were invisible, and so was the rest of her.

'That is so cool!' she gasped.

Fay smiled. 'Cool, but also useful when you need to be hidden. Well done. Now send it back and call the next.'

It was late by the time Linnet had learnt how to control all the different coloured Powers properly. Earth Power had entwined Fay and Arculus in thick grey-green ropes of Old Man's Beard creeper, and she had had trouble untangling them. Arculus had become quite vocal at being awoken from his sleep. And his teeth and claws had been just as alarming as Linnet had feared.

But it was the skyforce which had proven to be the hardest to control. Her tired mind had had trouble in grasping the thread, which slipped and slid away from her like a white will-o'-the-wisp. When she had eventually grasped it, first it had begun to snow gently and then, quite without warning, an absolute avalanche of hail had erupted from the top of the silver dome. Linnet had let go of the skyforce in a hurry as she emerged blue-lipped and bruised from the huge pile of hailstones that had buried her. She gritted her teeth and prepared to try again.

'Enough!' said Fay, laughing. 'I don't think Arculus would appreciate being buried in icebergs this time.'

'I wouldn't,' he growled. 'It's bad enough having to lick that creeper sap out of my fur.' So Linnet summoned the six strands of air back into the bottle as Fay showed her, and put it back in her pouch.

'You have done very well indeed, Linnet. You just need a little more practice. Your next lesson in Power will be with the Lady Rhiannon. You will know when it is time for it. Now, you should go home before your parents come back and worry about you. Arculus, the dome, please.' The cat sighed deeply, and as he did so the dome collapsed and disappeared into a silver-grey mouse shape, which he then chased round the room and swallowed whole.

'Oh, Arculus,' said Fay crossly. 'I wish you wouldn't do that.' The cat just grinned and licked his fangs with a long pink tongue.

Half an hour later, Linnet let herself into the quiet cottage. Her parents weren't back, and she went straight to bed. Perhaps this Maiden thing wasn't going to be too difficult after all, she thought. Apart from the hail, she had found the stuff she had learned tonight quite easy to do. That was encouraging, considering how hard she usually found learning things. And being invisible was going to be brilliant. Just wait till she told Petroc about that.

But just when she'd gone to sleep again after hearing her parents come in, she woke up screaming as the wyrm struck for the second time.

chapter eight

The Misery of Magret

Folk of the Earth
Folk of the Air,
Helpmates and counsel
In time of despair...

From 'The Prophecies of the Seven'

*M*agret Bickerspike had finally gone to bed. She had missed two perfectly good days of school for two whole wasted days of policewomen questioning her. It wasn't a good swap as far as she was concerned. Where had her brother gone? they'd asked. Had he had any problems (not him, not the golden University boy, thought Magret sourly)? Why did she think he'd taken the technomachine? Why had he decided to dig up Black Meadows? What were all the test-tubes in his room full of? On and on and on they went, until Magret's normally intelligent head felt like it was stuffed with a nest of snakes, curling and coiling question marks round her brain. How did she know? Tom never told her anything except boastful stories about the clever things he got up to at Oxenfoord.

Jem and Ada, the two old cousins who looked after her and the farm in termtime when Tom was away, had come rushing back when they heard the news. Stout Ada had fluttered around making cups of tea for the policewomen interviewing Magret, and Jem had got on with the farm business in his usual brusque, taciturn manner.

Magret bit the already soaked pillow to stifle her angry sobs. She hadn't cried at all since the police came, but tonight it had all got too much. Surely she didn't deserve this? Why did all these horrible things have to happen to her? It was bad enough, after all the family deaths, that Tom had done what he said he would, now that he could please himself, and gone off to Oxenfoord, leaving her all alone with boring Jem and Ada for months at a time in the terms. Why did he have to go and disappear as well?

He'll probably come back with some fancy explanation that lets him off scot free, she thought crossly. And then he'll go out and spend money on me, like he always does to say sorry and keep me quiet. He reckons he can buy me off with dresses and stuff – acting like he's Lord Bountiful or something, and I should be a grateful little girl. I'm not a little girl any more, in case he hasn't realised, and I can't be bothered with all that dressing up stuff, though I s'pose it's better than wearing charity-shop rags like Dad made me. I'd rather read a good book. But he never buys me one of those.

Magret sat up and snatched a tissue from the box beside her bed, blowing her bright red nose over and over in great honks till it hurt. Her anger and hurt at

Tom rose up again and overflowed in another burst of sobbing. He never takes any notice of me, she raged silently, except when I have Linnet over, and that's only because he wants to impress her with how great he is. It's pathetic. She's only just thirteen. But I s'pose he thinks it's funny the way she blushes when he comes in the room and teases her. Otherwise he's much more interested in his exciting new friends and their smart cars than in me and my life. Why can he not realise just how lonely I am in this big old farmhouse with no one to talk to properly?

She sniffled wetly as she lay down again, and punched the pillows hard. It just isn't fair, she wailed fiercely to herself, hot tears running down into her mouth. I miss Mum's hugs so dreadfully. Ada's like an old-fashioned bolster – stuffed full of straw and with about as much cosiness as one, and Jem's got the intelligence of a pitchfork. I want to go to University too, she thought, but Tom's as bad as Dad about listening on that subject. He expects me to work really hard at school, but then he says he reckons girls are better off staying at home, looking pretty and getting married. Well, I won't. I won't. I'll get away from here if it kills me.

She turned over onto her back and reached for another tissue to blow her sore nose again, thinking hard. Just what *had* Tom been doing spending time in his bedroom mixing up that smelly gloop he collected from Black Meadows all holidays? she wondered. He had said it would make their fortunes, but she didn't believe it. How could a load of mud be worth anything? And what had he been doing again in Black Meadows two nights ago?

She'd heard him slip out of the back door late, but just thought he was going to check that she'd locked the hens up. They'd had trouble with a fox a few evenings before, and lost some pullets. Then she'd fallen asleep and never heard him come home. Which he hadn't, of course.

'Typical that he thought I'd forget to lock up the hens,' she muttered out loud, a different kind of resentment washing over her as she remembered. 'He never thinks I can do anything practical. But I've built a nice little business out of those hens without any help from him. If he'd notice. Which he hasn't.' She went over the events of the previous day in her mind for the hundredth time – trying to make sense of them.

In the early morning had come the furious call from the technomachine hire company, and a short while after that, the police and their questions. Magret got out of bed and went over to the window. The moon was just past full, and she looked out over the still farmyard to the place where her brother had supposedly disappeared from with that wretched technomachine.

'I'm going to see right now,' she announced to the quiet room, glad to have made a decision – to be doing something herself. 'I'll bet he's out there somewhere avoiding everyone, stupid idiot. He probably drove the machine into the river or something and doesn't want to face the music.' She flung on her clothes and crept downstairs quickly, being careful to avoid touching the creaky bannisters. Her gumboots and jacket stood by the back door, and she put them on silently, lifted the latch and slipped out into the night air unnoticed. Ten minutes later, the mud of Black Meadows was sucking at her feet.

The moon was making rainbows on its surface, just as it had two nights before.

'Tom,' shouted Magret furiously. 'Tom Bickerspike! I hate you for doing this! Come on home this minute. I know you're out there somewhere. Coward! This is your sister!' But the mud remained dumb, keeping its secrets, and after a while, Magret grew hoarse and gave up calling for her brother. She began to walk towards the river Ash, drawn by the flicker of moonshine on its swift waters.

There was a slight ripple and tremble behind her as the mud suddenly moved and surged silently upwards, mounding up higher and higher, casting a long moonshadow in which a pair of red cateyes glowed. Pale green figures began to rise up and encircle the rearing earth in a dance of hopelessness, mouthing frantic spells of containment and binding. But the Queen of the Fey had been in the mortal world too long – she was almost too weak to dance the warning spells at all – the wyrm was awake and hungry again, and there was prey nearby, prey that smelled somewhat like its meal of two nights ago – but of anger and despair this time, not greed.

Magret reached the river Ash, knelt down and leaned over the water, soothed out of her anger at Tom for a moment by looking at her reflection framed by reeds and swaying weed. Perhaps she was a moongirl, she thought, distracted, her face soft and mysterious in the dark light. That was what her dad had used to call her when she'd gone off with her books – 'Moony Magret' – but it wasn't a compliment. She reached out a finger to touch the Magret-behind-the-water; the Magret whose eyes looked so much more knowing than her own; the Magret who in her preoccupation with her thoughts and her enchanted reflection, did not see or hear the worldwyrm rising up to kill again.

It raised one huge talon slightly and speared the moonstruck girl right through her torso. She didn't even have time to scream. The Magret-in-the-water disappeared in a shower of red blood-raindrops as the wyrm lifted her body to its mouth. But the Queen and her Fey Folk flew at its eyes, momentarily blinding it, and the body slid wetly off its talon and fell into the water with a splash, disappearing downstream in the fast-flowing current. The wyrm roared its frustration and its huge head thrashed and flailed until the whole valley was shaking with its anger. It surged towards the Bickerspike farmhouse and buildings, the Fey Folk and their exhausted Queen still flying containment spells round its head. It gorged on mouthfuls of brick and stone, and the tender, screaming human morsels within, which smelled of lost prey. It bolted a barn full of cows, a pen full of sheep and a hut full of Magret's hysterical hens. And finally sated when all was collapsed into ruin and destruction, it allowed the Fey Folk dancers to bind and quieten it with their weakened spells, and send it sliding silently back down into its resting place to digest its meal. For now.

Linnet was hoarse with horror and silent screaming. She could still see what was going on in Black Meadows even with her eyes open. 'Oh Magret, poor, poor Magret,' she choked, full of sorrow and grief for her friend. 'And that *thing*, that awful huge *thing*! How am I ever going to put *that* back to sleep?' She rocked herself on the bed, helpless and afraid as the house shook and rattled around her with the wyrm's fury. A thumping of footsteps came upstairs and along the corridor, and her door slammed open.

'Linnet,' said her father urgently. 'Linnet, come down into the garden. This is a big shake, and we'll be safer out there.' He bundled her into a blanket and down the stairs to where her mother was waiting, and then the three of them ran out of the back door. The peasticks had all fallen down and the appleblossom was floating through the air like pink snowflakes as the trees groaned and shook with the effort of keeping their roots in the ground. And then, abruptly, it all stopped.

'Ruddy technotonic plates,' growled Merrilin, looking up at the chimney, which was a lot more crooked than it had been before. There were tiles in the garden, and the small terrace wall had collapsed at one end. But Wyrmesbury was built very strongly, as well as wound round with powerful protective spells by the Guardians. It had been shaken on many occasions, and there was nothing that could not be repaired, given tools and time.

Linnet smiled weakly at him as he took her hand and her mother's and led them towards the kitchen for a restorative cup of tea. How could she tell him it wasn't technotonic plates? How could she tell him that a giant wyrm had just murdered her friend Magret, and destroyed the Bickerspike farm and all that lived there? It was then that she realised what it was to be a Guardian. Silence and secrecy and the protection of others – whatever the cost to yourself. It was not a notion a normal thirteen-year-old should have had, she thought. She felt doubly ashamed of her behaviour at school that morning.

'I'm OK, Dad,' she said, yawning exaggeratedly as they reached the bottom of the stairs. 'Tea will just wake me up more. It's stopped now, so I'm going back to bed again. Night, both of you.'

After she had hugged her parents and gone up to her room, she went over to her chest of drawers and pulled out Wayland's magical pouch. She was still rigid and horrified by the thought of what had happened to Magret, but she blocked it out determinedly, calling on Sunstar's Gift of courage to help her. There was no school tomorrow, and she knew her parents wouldn't wake her in the morning after the night's disturbance. She also knew, with an instinct that surprised her with its insistence, that it was time to call on the Lady Rhiannon and learn more about her Power. She got dressed in her most practical clothes – shirt, warm hoodie (her favourite pink one with 'Shakspear Rocks!' written on the back), jeans and her only dry pair of trainers. Then she took out the chain and the small silver horseshoe and hung them round her neck, putting her left hand on the tiny charm as she spoke.

'Daughter of Mares, I have need of speed to bring me to you,' she said, going over to the window and opening it. A cloud covered the moon briefly and then galloped towards her, forming itself into a bucking, tossing horse shape made of nothing but mist and air. It rushed into the small room, bringing with it the smell of cold, high places. 'Oh well,' said Linnet, climbing onto its back, which was surprisingly comfortable. 'I can't ride, but I don't suppose it matters. Please will you take me to your mistress?' Almost as she spoke, they hurtled into the air again, over the Badger's mound and away to Rinnon's Crest, where Rhiannon and her birds were waiting.

'Come, Maiden,' said Rhiannon, mounting the snorting cloud horse behind her. 'Let us go and consult the small folk of Earth and Air. You have a Choice to make.'

It was a wild, wild flight. As they rode, Rhiannon taught Linnet the finer points of riding the wind and controlling its breath. It was a lesson that took forever and no time at all, but finally Linnet took over the reins from her with confidence and gave the signal for the little cloud horse to descend. Long grey breakers crashed on rocky seaweed sands, and beyond them a rugged land where everything looked somehow larger and more dangerous than the soft rounded landscape of home. The cloud horse landed at the foot of a great mountain slope where boulders lay strewn like giants' doorstops. The sky grew dark and cloudy as Rhiannon's birds whistled warningly and scattered into a hole in the rocks.

'Step carefully here, Maiden,' said Rhiannon, 'for we are on the border of the overlands of the wolf goddess who is called Nemain Stormcrow, and the underkingdom of Caebrolla the Nimble and her folk of Earth and Air. Nemain is an old enemy of mine, and she is not gentle with trespassers, so we must pass by her door quietly, but my birds have warned the dwarf queen of our presence, and she will be expecting us.'

Linnet took a firmer grip on Wayland's pouch and picked her way slowly behind Rhiannon up the rocky path towards the top of the mountain. She wanted to ask questions, but her newly awakened Maiden memories told her firmly to keep silent. She thought that it might be wise to listen to them. What they were saying about Nemain was not nice at all.

All of a sudden they came before two great grey dolmenstones on either side of the path, both as tall as a house, and pointing up like huge fingers at the clouds above. In the centre of each was set a brass bell above a hammer, and some letters carved underneath. Rhiannon stopped, and Linnet moved past her to read them. On the left-hand stone was written 'Nemain's Domain' and on the right 'Caebrolla's Cave'. The right-hand stone also had a slate propped up against it with some words chalked on it in old-fashioned curly script:

Girls and Goddesses welcome (mostly).
Boys and Gods tolerated.
Absolutely no travelling salesmen or Fey Folk.
By Order

'Nemain is most certainly to be avoided – her bite is much worse than her howl. Caebrolla is the one we need,' said Rhiannon in a low voice. She took the small hammer and banged loudly on Caebrolla's bell. As she did so, a flap snapped open low down in the stone.

'What do you want?' boomed a woman's voice.

'I am Rhiannon, the Daughter of Mares and I bring news and the Maiden.'

'Ah,' said the voice more softly, and the stone split wide to reveal a tiny, very broad woman with long brown hair, dressed in a warrior's blue tunic. It had small skulls dangling from it. She looked Linnet up and down. 'So you're that one. Caebrolla is waiting for you. You'd best come in before Nemain catches you. She doesn't like Maidens or goddesses. In fact she doesn't like anyone.'

They followed the dwarf woman down a long and winding stair, deep into the earth. After a long time they emerged into a large cavern. There were benches all around the edge, and on the benches sat hundreds of dwarven warriors, both male and female, polishing shields, skulls and spears and chatting noisily to one another. At the end of the cavern was a throne made of sparkling crystal, which lit the whole place like a beacon. Sitting on the throne was a short person who could only be Caebrolla, Linnet thought. She was covered in birds and small winged beasts from head to foot, and their singing voices combined with the chatter of the warriors to make a tremendous din that echoed round and round the cavern. Linnet flung up her hands and covered her ears against the sudden and overwhelming flood of languages. Incredibly, she understood all of them, and they competed against each other in her head – strange sounding words jostling and bumping until she thought she would scream with the effort of keeping them all separate. The movement caught the woman's eye. She looked up and whistled shrilly, once. The noise stopped immediately, and she beckoned Linnet towards the throne.

'Welcome to my cave, Maiden,' she said, smiling at her. 'Rhiannon's birds brought me and my Air folk news of your coming. We are pleased that your Choosing brings you here.'

Mocker, Bluejay and Bough flew back to Rhiannon's shoulder as Caebrolla bowed. 'Welcome, Daughter of Mares. It has been long and long since you visited us.' Rhiannon bowed back, her long silver hair falling forward to touch the cave floor.

'It has been long and long, but now the worldwyrm is moving again, and the Maiden needs a guide to lead her through Avvallon. Will you folk of Earth and Air help?' Caebrolla nodded slowly.

'We have much to discuss together, Rhiannon. Let the Maiden go to the kitchens until we are done – a lot has happened to her today, and she looks hungry.' Linnet's stomach gave a loud growl. It was true – so much had happened to her on this long, eventful day – the disaster of calling the bees at school, Petroc's anger, learning to control Fay's Gift, and Rhiannon's. She realised she had forgotten to eat for most of it, and that her stomach was telling her that it was starving, but she resented being sent off like unwanted baggage. As she opened her mouth to say so, the dwarf queen looked at her understandingly – and it seemed to Linnet that she had an urgent question in her eyes.

'Use your Power,' said Caebrolla. 'Follow your nose, Maiden and ask your Maiden memories. It is important for us all that you Choose rightly.' With this cryptic utterance, she turned back to Rhiannon, leaving Linnet with nothing else to do but follow her command.

Linnet stumbled through a maze of stone passages in the direction her nose and stomach told her to go. She still felt as if she were dreaming. A picture of Magret's torn and bloody body floated before her. That was something else that had happened today. She knew – all too well now – that it was real, but she still couldn't think of it without wanting to scream and cry and hide from the fact of it. She shuddered, remembering that her friend would never be hungry again. And now she was in a place that should only exist in fairytales. She asked herself yet again why this sort of thing happened to Linnet Perry – a girl who only this morning – or was it yesterday morning by now? – had gone to school on the bus with Petroc Suleymann in the ordinary way? As she stepped through an archway into a wall of noise, she had come up with no useful answer. Her Power lay dormant – a small, hot sun inside her – and her Maiden memories were silent for the moment.

Caebrolla's kitchen was large and full of warmth, and much too real to be a dream. It had an arched roof where bundles of herbs and hams and other good things hung, it seemed to be full of dwarf warriors cooking, eating and talking, all at the tops of their voices. She slipped onto the end of a bench covered in dishes of good things and found that Caebrolla and her stomach had been right. She was indeed starving. She helped herself again and again until she was so full she couldn't move. This was definitely better than toast and curled up old ham.

When she had finished, she turned and looked around her. What was it Caebrolla had said about choosing rightly? Choosing what? Or whom? Come on, she thought at her Power crossly. Help me. The small hot sun flared and glowed at once, and her eye fell on a dwarf sitting by the fireside, playing a small silver harp. He had one of the strange winged beasts tattooed on his right arm, and a cheerful face behind a bristling blue beard that fell halfway down his chest. And he was different from the other dwarves in the kitchen. He was the only one who had long purplish pointed ears that twitched slightly at the tips. She felt that she liked him immediately – but more importantly, there was something about him that drew her. Her Power pulsed again as she stared at him intently. She knew she needed this dwarf, even if she didn't know why yet. It was time to do as Caebrolla had said and ask.

Well? she demanded silently of her Maiden memories. What's special about him? Who is he? Why should I Choose him? The door in her mind opened invitingly, and as she closed her eyes a series of images poured out of it. First came a castle with a legendary king and queen sitting under the snapping banners of a tournament and before them a small blue-bearded harper, playing. Linnet knew at once who the king and queen were and where – she had loved the stories of Artur Mac Uthair and Jennivere from when she was very young and now it seemed that in some small way they were connected to her own story. A small spark of pleasure at this thought began to burn inside her as the images changed, and she saw Maidens flying through the air on the back of strange beasts, Maidens lulled by music, Maidens laughing, Maidens beset by danger – and in every image they were accompanied by a dwarf with a bright blue beard and a harp.

Abruptly the Power interrupted and sent a name and another picture into her mind. It was time to act. Linnet stood up and moved across the crowded kitchen, still somewhat unsure of herself, but determined anyway. As she did so, the dwarf's magnificent beard seemed to vibrate to some unseen signal and he looked straight up at her with one green and one blue eye, just like her own. Now she was absolutely sure, and the Power seized her voice and spoke through her. Inside her head, the Maidens applauded.

'Mathafurd Llewellyn, harper of Earth and Air,' said Linnet, and her voice rang out across all the noise and chatter with a depth and authority it had never had before. 'You are found and Chosen by the Maiden. I summon you in the name of Artur Mac Uthair and Jennivere, before whom you played at Cammelott, to guide and protect till summer's lease or worldwyrm end.' The unusual words died away and she was just Linnet again. But she felt different. She felt like the Maiden for the first time.

Mathafurd Llewellyn bowed deeply and started towards her, harp in hand. But suddenly his beard started to fizz with rainbow sparks.

'Ah,' he said, 'the Queen too summons . . . she has her own ways of knowing! Come!' And with that, he made for the entrance, scattering dwarves and cooking pots as he went.

Linnet knew she had to follow him. She had to run, for despite his small size, she needed to take two strides to every one of his. In no time at all, they were in the great cavern of the crystal throne once more. Caebrolla and Rhiannon were again surrounded by birds, winged beasts, warriors and weapons and noise, but as soon as Linnet ran in they beckoned her over.

'Did you find what you sought in the kitchens and make

your Choice?' Caebrolla asked – and the question hung in the air as if it was the most important thing in the world.

'Yes,' said Linnet slowly, looking over at the dwarf she had followed. 'Yes, I did. I found *him*. Your harper. The one with eyes like mine. And I Chose him too.' As she pointed him out, her voice rang with Power, and Caebrolla nodded in a satisfied way.

'The Maiden has sought and Chosen, and as it always has been in the past so it is now. It is a true finding, and so a rightful Choosing,' said Caebrolla, and her voice echoed and rang like a battle horn, silencing the noisy cave utterly. 'I have spoken with the Daughter of Mares and it is time for the folk of Earth and Air to act again to aid the Maiden. Mathafurd Llewellyn, come forth.'

The dwarf who Linnet had found in the kitchens stepped forward, and stood at Linnet's side as Caebrolla continued.

'Once more you and your companion beast Gladysant will stand ready to guard and guide this Maiden through Avvallon when she asks it of you. For from now on her task is yours and your paths will lie together, as they have before with other Maidens, until the worldwyrm is laid to rest. Let us hope it is forever this time.'

As she heard Caebrolla's words falling like fateful stones into the silence around her, Linnet opened her mouth, then shut it again, clenching her teeth against apologies she knew would be pointless. This Power business was obviously going to take some getting used to. Was this going to happen every time she was drawn to someone? What happened if she had to Choose Petroc for some awful task? Or her mum? Or dad? Were they going to be affected by this Power of hers? Look at what had just happened. Her Power had spoken through her, words she couldn't control had tumbled from her lips, and now a complete stranger's life had been utterly disrupted because of the Choice she had made. No matter that the poor dwarf had apparently done this who knows how many times in the past – and that it seemed to be his destiny, like being the Maiden was hers – she trusted her Maiden memories that this was true. But nevertheless, now she had Chosen a guard and guide to take her to a place she'd never heard of until last night – a place that to the real world didn't even exist – *and he had to come with her whether he wanted to or not.* She wouldn't blame him if he wanted to go there as little as she did. Perhaps she should apologise after all, she thought uncertainly . . .

She turned to him, looking into the blue and green eyes so like her own and immediately felt safe and comforted. There was no need for apologies. Her Maiden memories whispered inside her head and reassured her that Mathafurd Llewellyn had the sort of spirit which craved any kind of adventure, however dangerous. Linnet whispered back that she just wished hers did. Then it suddenly occurred to her that another name had been mentioned – a companion beast. That sounded a bit scary – a beast. She opened her mouth to ask Mathafurd who and what Gladysant was – and where. But Rhiannon was beckoning her urgently up the passage and it seemed that the moment for questions and explanations had passed for now.

'Thank you,' she said instead, turning her head. 'At least you've done this before so you might know what you're doing. Which is more than I seem to,' she muttered under her breath.

The dwarf chuckled. 'That remains to be seen,' he said. 'Meanwhile, Gladysant and I are entirely at your service, Maiden. We will take you home to Wyrmesbury. It will be strange to see it again after so long.'

As they left Caebrolla's Cave, Mathafurd Llewellyn followed them out, closing the stone door behind them with a dull clunk. While Rhiannon mounted the cloud horse again, Linnet glanced across the stone path at Nemain Stormcrow's front door. Sitting in front of it now was a very beautiful lady dressed in black, but as she caught Linnet looking she growled and changed into a great snarling wolf, which lunged forward but was suddenly brought up short by an invisible barrier halfway across the pathway. Rhiannon laughed – a nervous horse whinny. 'And good day to you too, Nemain,' she said bravely. Mathafurd Llewellyn just snorted.

'Go away, you hairy old monster,' he said. 'You can't cross Caebrolla's border and you don't frighten me none, 'cause I've got a better beast of my own.' Then he plucked a fizzing rainbow hair from his beard and poked it at the tattoo on his right arm. 'Wake up, Gladysant, my dear,' he called, and immediately the tattoo began to coil and grow, pouring like smoke onto the ground and becoming solid as it did so.

Soon a winged beast stood there – Mathafurd's tattoo made reality. She had an eared eagle's head, a spotted leopard's body, the hooves of a deer (eight of them), not to mention a dragon's tail and huge wings covered in feathers as pink as a cloud at sunrise. A sound like the belling of hounds rumbled out, not from her beak, but from her belly. As Mathafurd scrambled onto her back with considerable difficulty, the belling changed to complaining whines. The dwarf held a hand out for Linnet, who at once had a vivid and irrepressible vision of her mother's face if she should see them landing in the vegetable garden. Despite everything, it suddenly seemed terribly funny to think of her un-Wyrmesbury mother face to face with a pink-winged monster.

'I think,' snorted Linnet, trying unsuccessfully not to giggle at her thoughts as she settled herself behind him, 'that we'd better not hide you two in the potting shed. My mum might not like it very much.'

'I think,' said Mathafurd, grinning through his beard at her, 'that you may very well be right. Gladysant and I will find a more dignified place to rest ourselves than this "potting shed". Nice though it sounds,' he added politely, as Gladysant's belly barked in agreement.

'The Smith awaits you, Maiden,' said Rhiannon, bringing them back into the present moment again. 'He has a lesson to teach. There is little time and much for you to learn. I shall go and do what must be done for the girl Magret's body.' Yet again, Linnet couldn't bear to think of the pale, soaked, bloodless figure that had been her friend floating in the River Ash. It was just too hard – too much, even with her new sense of responsibility. So she blocked out the horrid vision once more and concentrated on staying on Gladysant's furry back. The pink wings beat through the air again and again, and the journey back to Wyrmesbury took no time at all, it seemed, as Mathafurd talked to her of Maidens past, and told her stories of the deeds of Artur and Lancelet and Bediver and the Knights of the Round Table in his slow deep voice that sounded like singing. Soon they had landed outside Wayland Smith's forge. She said goodbye to Mathafurd, patted Gladysant's slightly damp beak and watched as they leapt back into the midnight sky.

'Gladysant and I will wait for you on Hootcat Hill at the door to Avvallon,' called a disembodied voice from above.

'Hopefully you'll be waiting a good long while,' muttered Linnet as she waved goodbye. 'Because that's the last place I want to go right now. And the longer I can put off meeting that Fey sorceress, the better.'

There was a clashing and a banging from the back of the forge as she pushed the big double doors open.

'Wayland Smith!' she shouted into the smoke and flame. 'Oi! Wayland Smith! I'm here for my lesson!' But as usual when Wayland was working, there was no answer, so she seized a small thread of Power and sent it out to poke him in the ribs.

It got his attention almost immediately. He dropped the hammer he was working with and swore loudly. Then he turned round and saw her.

'Linnet Perry,' he said crossly. 'The Power is not to be used for poking people.'

She grinned up at him, unafraid. 'So what are you going to do – turn me into a toad?'

He grinned back, his momentary temper gone at once. 'No – but I'll teach you to hide in a spark! Will that do instead?' At once he muttered a spell Linnet couldn't quite hear, and disappeared. All that was left in the gloomy air was a bright spark, that drifted towards her and settled on her shoulder, glowing and warming her neck.

'Now you do it,' said a tiny, fiery voice in her ear.

'How?' asked Linnet. The spark sighed gustily, nearly extinguishing itself.

'The spell is . . .

> 'O choinneal geal na hAislinge
> Lig an tsoilse beag amach.
> O bright dream candle,
> Let out a tiny light.'

Linnet took a deep breath and repeated the Smith's words. At once she felt sparkly and hot with Power. She floated through the air, sizzling.

'That,' said Wayland Smith, returning to himself, 'was impressive. Now say the spell in reverse and turn back.'

But try as she might, Linnet remained a spark.

Wayland sighed again. 'I knew it was too good to be true,' he said mournfully. 'Maidens these days. They're just not as good as they used to be.'

Linnet felt a hot, furious flare of anger infuse her currently tiny being. How dare he? After all that had been said about her being the most Powerful Maiden ever. Had they all been lying to her? Was she useless after all? No! said her Maiden memories. Of course she was just as good as any Maiden who had ever lived. Better in fact! Then Linnet saw what Wayland had been trying to do. Her anger had focussed her and made her stronger. She muttered the reverse spell again, correctly this time, and popped back into her own body.

'You knew that would happen!' she said accusingly.

The Smith just smiled infuriatingly and waggled his grimy eyebrows at her. 'Now do it again,' he said.

Linnet stuck her tongue out at him, but she did it anyway, just to show she could.

chapter nine

Missing Persons

*'The mouthless dead across your dreams
in pale battalions go . . .'*

Charles Sorley

Fidget Reedglitter stood at the Door and tapped one pointed tooth with a long green fingernail. Seven mortal years were nearly up and the Changeover was upon them again. The Fey Prince and his guards were ready to leave Avvallon through the Door and take up their duties in Black Meadows. But more importantly, the returning Queen would need to be restored to health as a matter of urgency after her long sojourn in the mortal world. First of all, her beautiful Fey form must be renewed with a drop of the magical dragonwort elixir from the Chalice of Athyr, which Fidget had already retrieved from its watery hiding place. Then there should be music, music to take her mind off the misery of the ages-old enforced separation from her beloved Prince, which always hit her hard whenever she passed in or out of her kingdom and met him on the way with no time for more than a fleeting kiss of greeting. The Queen would have no heart for dancing yet. She had done enough of that in the mortal world lately, from what Fidget had seen in her crystal ball.

Yes, the music must come first, before even a banquet and a Hunt. But what kind of music? The old Fey sorceress picked up a small silver horn and smiled, stroking the metal with long bony fingers. It was not a kind smile. A mortal musician, she thought. A mortal musician would do nicely. They hadn't had one of those for a long time – since that wretched Tam Lynn had escaped her clutches, in fact. A captive mortal might make the Queen feel better about the fast-waning Power of old magic and her lost Prince. Make her forget for a while that for every mortal year she spent in the human world guarding that blasted wyrm, her beautiful body was punished, decaying and dwindling to nothing but transparent green mist. Fidget spat, then raised the horn to her old, wrinkled lips and began to blow as she floated upwards. Mortals, she thought contemptuously as she opened the Door to Avvallon with a flick of her mind. They had been nothing but trouble from the beginning of time.

Inigo's Weir lay still and calm in the first light of dawn. Wedged against it, a pale, bloodless hand, attached to the pale, bloodless body of Magret Bickerspike waved aimlessly through the underwater weed. Back and forth, back and forth, greeting the early mist. The sound of hooves galloping broke the silence, as a white horse appeared quite suddenly on the bank of the river Ash. The mist shimmered, and the body disappeared for a moment, only to reappear cradled in the arms of a tall woman with long silver hair. 'Come, poor child,' whispered Rhiannon. 'You must rest in a better place than this.' A door opened in the air beside her, and she stepped through into nothingness.

At the same moment, a horn sounded on Hootcat Hill, summoning, summoning. Its eerie calling music floated over the fields to Wyrmesbury and wove its way into the ears of a sleeping girl. She picked up her 'cello and made her way silently down Gold Street, face vacant and yearning with an unfulfilled longing to make her own instrument sing with that unearthly tune. Its silvered notes drifted on over Black Meadows, and for those with eyes to see, a malignant green form floated down towards Wyrmesbury behind the music, landing for a moment and then compelling the unknowing, unseeing girl and the 'cello with it, up into the air and down again to Hootcat Hill and back through the Door, which closed behind them with a snap.

'Welcome to Avvallon, mortal girl,' said Fidget Reedglitter nastily. 'Now play for me.'

In the ordinary world, where wyrms and fairies and magical tunes were things that happened in children's stories and could therefore have absolutely no credible involvement with a crime scene, the Vesterton police were baffled and, frankly, annoyed. The Bickerspike farm had been nothing but trouble to them lately. First there had been the business of Young Tom and the stolen digger, and now the place seemed to have been flattened and destroyed by a freak whirlwind in the middle of the night. What other explanation could there possibly be? But it meant hours of early morning paperwork and filing of missing persons reports, for no sign could be found of Jem and Ada Bickerspike, nor of the girl Magret.

'They must have been sucked up and taken,' said the sergeant to his constable, chewing his pen. 'It happens in Amerika all the time.' And Fay Morgan, who happened to have come calling for some of Magret's eggs (or so she said), nodded and agreed. The fact that she was muttering frantic spell words of diversion and distraction beneath her breath escaped the two policemen totally. Which was, of course, the point.

Petroc lay in his bed, considering things. Sleep was impossible since the last earth tremor, and he'd had a terrible nightmare about Linnet and Magret that he couldn't quite remember now. It wasn't that which was worrying him most, though. It was Linnet herself. He was still finding it hard to get his head round what had happened at school yesterday – the magic she had done so casually – apparently without any thought for the consequences till afterwards.

Petroc felt a bit bad about being cross and distant with her – shutting her out, he supposed – but right now he didn't have any idea how to deal with this new sort of best friend who could call killer bees out of thin air, talk to everything that lived, and – almost worse – who had this great and terrible quest which didn't seem to include him in any way. He was the sort of person who needed time to think – to ponder things and come to terms with them. Reacting quickly came as second nature on the football field or the cricket pitch, but this sort of stuff was totally alien to him. He didn't know how to react to the new Linnet yet, and he didn't like it.

Perhaps, he thought rather guiltily, it was because all this magical Maiden stuff made her seem so much more important than him all of a sudden, and he didn't like that much, if he was honest – didn't like being left out of it, either. Their friendship had always been really vital to his entire life – Linn was good at making him laugh, teasing him about his seriousness and his sporting prowess and, most important of all, always doing *everything* with him. But ever since they'd been small he'd been the stronger one of the two – Linnet's protector, her rescuer, her comforter, the ultimate decision maker. He was the one she came running to when she was in trouble – him or Magret. Now, in the space of the few days he'd been visiting his gran, things had gone all topsy-turvy. He was still just a schoolkid, but Linnet had morphed into someone he suddenly didn't understand at all – someone who probably didn't need him anymore, he thought bitterly.

Yes, as far as he could see she could protect herself perfectly well now without him, and if she couldn't do it then she'd choose others to. Magical others. And where did that leave him? Nowhere, Petroc decided, and he still didn't like the feeling at all. It wasn't normal. It wasn't safe. It made him feel small, afraid and useless, and it tapped into the part of his Wyrmesbury heritage he had deliberately put off thinking about properly all his life –

the having-magical-blood part that they all joked about in the family, but which he now knew was probably truth after yesterday. He'd felt Linnet's Power as she called it – he'd heard those blasted bees before they erupted out of nowhere. Normal humans couldn't do that. He was sure of it.

Cursing the Wyrmesbury ancestors who had left him with this unwanted legacy, he got out of bed and decided to go and see if his sister Zafira was awake this early. Perhaps she'd want to play him her latest 'cello piece – the concerto by the Russkian – Cajkovskij she called him, or something like that. Her playing always calmed him down and helped him think more clearly.

Twenty minutes later, Petroc stood panting at the foot of the stairs, his voice hoarse with calling, and his calf muscles burning with running up and down the stairs and into every room in the house. Zafira had disappeared without a trace and her 'cello with her. He just knew she wouldn't have gone out with her instrument this early. 'Cellos didn't do well in the damp, and the morning mist was still on the streets. She wouldn't have risked ruining it. Was this something to do with Linnet? Had the wyrm taken his sister like it took Young Tom? He wrenched open the front door, and pelted through the streets, taking the short cuts across to the eastern edge of Wyrmesbury, leaping over the Perrys' back garden, skirting the rubble of the wall, until he was under Linnet's window. He threw a clod of earth up. Missed. Threw another. And another. Finally, the window opened and a very tousled head peered out.

'What?' it said, blearily.

'M . . . M . . . Mr Perry,' he stammered. 'I was looking for Linnet.'

'So was I,' said Merrilin in a worried voice. 'She's not in her bed, and Nyneve had a dreadful nightmare about her being in danger near Black Meadows. I wouldn't take any notice, but there have been a lot of strange things going on lately, and Nyneve never dreams unless it's really important.'

'I dreamt about her too,' said Petroc, his own nightmare rushing back into his head. 'Her and Magret. And now Zafira's disappeared with her 'cello.'

'We'll come down,' said Merrilin, his head disappearing back into the house. As the back door opened, Petroc heard a faint, aggrieved howling coming from Hootcat Hill.

'What on earth is that?' he asked.

'Nothing of earth, I think. Best not to ask right now,' said Merrilin, grabbing a coat as Nyneve appeared in the doorway behind him. 'Nyneve and I will go down to Black Meadows and look for Linnet.'

'I dreamed about Magret too,' said Nyneve. 'But it's too horrible to be real. It just can't be. And Linnet . . .' She shook her head in denial, not wanting to think about what she'd seen Linnet doing. 'Wretched Wyrmesbury. I sometimes wish I'd never come here. It's all so *abnormal*,' she said crossly.

'Never mind abnormal. Wyrmesbury is how it is, Nyneve. You've known that for years. If Linnet and Magret are in danger, we have to go. Now. And never mind your quibbling. You know that perfectly well,' Merrilin replied curtly. He turned to Petroc. 'You wait for us here, in case Linnet comes back. We'll be as quick as we can.'

'Have some toast while you wait, Petroc,' said Nyneve in a last ditch attempt to bring some sort of normality into the conversation. 'If there's any bread that is,' she muttered distractedly.

'But what about Zafira?' Petroc asked urgently. 'My sister might be in danger too, if you remember.'

'We'll keep an eye out for her as well,' said Nyneve over her shoulder, running towards the small car where Merrilin was already revving the engine.

Petroc was far too anxious to eat toast. He paced the garden, thinking again. Linnet's parents didn't know anything about the Maiden stuff, or the Guardians or anything. At least, he didn't think they did. He just didn't know what to do. His gran was so ill, he didn't want to worry his parents, but if Zafira didn't come back . . . and where was Linnet? Had she disappeared too?

He sat down on the garden bench, put his head in his hands and groaned. He felt powerless and small again – not the usual confident football hero at all, who took care of everything and everyone. He had no magic – unless all this suddenly made his so-called magical blood wake up and do something spectacular, which seemed unlikely. What use was he to her or anyone in all this? Then all thought left him and he screamed hoarsely, as he felt something warm and alive press against his leg.

'I shan't bite,' said a voice, crossly, into his mind.

Petroc opened one eye cautiously and saw the warm, whiskery muzzle of Sunstar the Badger. 'Did you really say that?' he asked.

Sunstar snorted. 'Why is it you wyzard-blood mortals can never believe what you hear nowadays?' he asked. 'Of course it was me. Linnet is with Wayland Smith. If you want to find out about your sister, you'd better get over there, quickly. Now hurry!' And his squat body turned and disappeared through the gap in the hedge, running awkwardly towards the River.

It was a sign of how worried Petroc was that he simply accepted that a badger had spoken to him and didn't once consider how strange it was. He didn't even register the wyzard-blood comment either. Since he'd heard about Nyneve's dream, his mind was entirely focussed on getting to Linnet and Wayland Smith. Nothing else mattered. It seemed that Linnet was all right, at least for now, but he *had* to find out what had happened to Zafira. He leapt back over the ruined wall and pelted down the streets, hardly noticing their emptiness and tranquillity in the face of his determination to get there as fast as possible. His long legs worked harder than they had ever done on a pitch, and he hurtled round corners and across roads without any consideration for his own safety. His breath started to come in short gasps, and the sweat dripped down his face, soaking his shirt, and he had to slow down a bit at the last steep hill. 'Come on,' he panted. 'Come on,' and with a last huge effort he covered the last bit of ground, sprinted towards Wayland Smith's workshop, banged on the doors and stumbled through them. There were Linnet and the Smith, sharing a cup of early morning tea.

Petroc ran straight to Linnet and hugged her hard. He found that he was really really glad to see her. 'You're safe,' he croaked. 'Thank everything, you're safe.' Linnet was hugging him back, sweat and all, when Wayland spoke.

'Just why didn't you think she was safe?'

Linnet pulled back from him. 'And how did you know I was here?' she asked 'What's happened?'

Petroc grabbed Linnet's tea and took a long gulp to wet his parched and panting throat. Then he looked at them both – he was scared and he wanted answers now. 'The badger sent me. And Zafira's disappeared with her 'cello. *Where is she?*' It came out in a hoarse shout.

'Whoa!' said the Smith, putting his huge hands on Petroc's shoulders. 'Calm down. Tell us what's happened. Then we can try and give you some answers.'

Linnet wriggled past Wayland's shoulder and grabbed Petroc's hand. 'Yes, tell us, 'Roc. We're all in this together now.' It was absolutely what Petroc needed to hear, and soon his story had been poured into their ears.

The Smith scratched his head. 'Doesn't sound like wyrm's work to me,' he said. Then he went silent, listening intently. 'I wonder . . .' he muttered. 'Linnet, fetch down that parcel wrapped in green – the one on the shelf at the back. There's something I want to try.' When Linnet touched it, the thing under the green velvet cloth buzzed and vibrated under her fingers, and she gasped as she felt its Power. Her Maiden memories buzzed and twittered as they told her what it was.

'Now,' said Wayland. 'Unwrap it, Linnet, and let's have a look.' It turned out to be a small silver mirror, very bright, with strange shifting patterns that strayed over the surface. He held it out to Linnet, formally. 'Take this

Feyglass,' he said. 'Look into it and show me what you See, Maiden.'

Linnet opened her mind to the Smith, looked, and immediately they both Saw – pictures swirling through time in a jumbled mass. It was hard to make sense of them.

Linnet squinted. There was someone who was obviously the Queen of the Fey Folk, tall and destructively beautiful in her own land and quite different from the green wispy thing Linnet had seen in Black Meadows. She was drinking from a golden chalice held by an ancient crone. Linnet shuddered at the evil expression on the crone's face.

'Is . . . is that Fidget Reedglitter?' she asked.

Wayland nodded. 'Using the dragonwort elixir illegally to boost the Queen's strength, it looks like to me. Must be just before she came over to our side the last time for the Changeover. Yes, see, it's altering now.'

Two processions of Fey Folk, passing each other, one, led by the Queen, vibrant and beautiful, her green body dressed in silks and jewels; the other, led by the Fey Prince, tarnished, transparent and wan at the mortal side of the Door to Avvallon. Wayland and Linnet watched them exchange one long kiss, before the Queen disappeared through the Door to take up her duty.

'I feel sorry for her,' said Linnet. 'It must be awful for her, only seeing her husband for a moment.'

'I wouldn't feel too sorry about that,' said Wayland. 'She manages. And it's her fault we're all in this mess in the first place.' The picture swirled and changed again, and Linnet cried out in anguish. Petroc held her hand tightly. It was all he could do. The Feyglass was just a mass of swirling mist to him, though he felt the Power rolling off it in waves.

'Do you see Zafira yet?' he whispered.

'No,' Linnet wept, 'no.' Tears poured down her face as she Saw, once again, the Fey Folk, desperately coaxing the worldwyrm back to its bed after Magret's death, and heard the shrill Fey voices, lamenting their loss of Power. 'They'll never keep it down,' she whimpered. 'They're too weak.' Then the picture changed again.

'Watch the Queen,' said Wayland. 'She's telling them it's time to go home.' Linnet Saw the Fey Queen's mortalworld body faded and wispy as green smoke, then heard her dull, cracked tones commanding her people to return with her for the Changeover. 'Sweet music and feasting await us,' she rasped. 'We leave today for Avvallon – let the wyrm wake as it wills. The Prince's power must tame it, for I can no longer dance the spells of sleeping.'

'Oh dear,' said Wayland as the picture changed for the last time. 'I thought so.'

Linnet groaned as she saw Zafira, beside the same wrinkled Fey crone, who was watching her with a malicious smile. She was sitting on a flowery mound, playing her 'cello with fingers that flew like demon wings. Her eyes were blank and empty in her dark face, and a thin thread of music seeped out of the mirror into the workshop.

'That's Zafira's piece,' Petroc gasped.

'And that's what I feared,' said Wayland Smith.

'What?' said Petroc. 'What did you fear? *I can't see what's happening! Tell me!*' Wayland sighed, beginning to pace round the workshop.

'It's not good news, but I don't think she will come to any harm. Zafira has been stolen and taken to Avvallon by Fidget Reedglitter to play for the Fey Queen on her return.

'Where's Avva — whatever it's called? Hey, Linnet, isn't that . . . isn't that where you have to go to get that stuff for defeating the wyrm?' Petroc's voice fell into silence.

'Yes, 'Roc. That's where I have to go, probably very soon. But I will rescue Zafira — I promise,' she said. Wayland stopped his pacing and began to speak again.

'Today is the time of Changeover, when the Fey Prince takes over the burden of guarding the wyrm. It could not have come at a worse moment. Because it means that as well as everything else you, Linnet, will have to find a way to seal Avvallon against the Queen's return.'

'Why? Why can't this Changeover just go ahead anyway?' asked Linnet. Her Maiden memories weren't helping at all on this one, and she felt confused. She had no idea how she was going to seal the Door to Avvallon against the Queen — or indeed why it was necessary.

'Look, Linnet. At the exact moment the Fey Queen returns, Fidget Reedglitter will summon the Chalice of Athyr and the dragonwort elixir from wherever they are hidden. You will have absolutely no chance of stealing them once they are back in her hands. Not only that, but the Queen will drink the elixir in order to return to her full power. Then you'll have none to put the worldwyrm back to sleep. You'll have to seal the Door in order to give yourself time.'

'But won't that make the Fey really angry? And what if the Fey Prince is waiting around on the other side? What then?' Linnet asked.

Wayland put his arm round her. 'I'm not going to lie. It will make the Fey very angry on both sides of the Door, and it will be very dangerous, because if they rebel or fail, the wyrm will lie unguarded and unchecked without the Feypower to contain it, and soon it will be hungry again. As for the Prince – he won't set out until the Queen does. Time works differently in Avvallon. If you go very soon, I think you will be safe – or as safe as you can be.'

'It's time for me to be the Maiden, isn't it?' asked Linnet in a rather small voice. She supposed she was going to be seeing Mathafurd and Gladysant again sooner than she had thought. The Smith sighed once more.

'Yes, there's no help for it, you must go to Hootcat Hill at once, Linnet. The Owlman will be waiting to help you and the dwarf into Avvallon. There is no more time, and I fear for your parents in Black Meadows. Petroc and I must go to them as soon as we can.'

'But what about Zafira?' Petroc cried angrily. 'My sister's in some weird otherworld place, and you aren't *doing* anything to save her!'

The Smith put his hand on Petroc's shoulder again. 'Nothing can be done for Zafira until Linnet has achieved what she must. But Zafira will not be harmed – musicians are much respected by the Fey – and she won't remember anything that has happened to her if all goes well. You will have to trust Linnet to get her out when the time is right. Now come with me. I must get you and Linnet's parents away to a safe place – I just hope they've come back by now. Anyone connected to the Maiden is in danger. There is no doubt now that the wyrm will rise again soon, and the Guardians must do what they can to contain it if the

Fey Folk are no longer willing or able. It won't be much, but we must try,' he said ruefully.

Three on a motorbike was both risky and difficult. Petroc and Linnet clung on to each other and leaned into the corners as Wayland Smith drove fast through the twisty streets, blue exhaust fumes billowing behind them on the quiet air of what was still very early morning despite all that had happened. As they drew up outside the Perry cottage, all Linnet's hard won confidence evaporated once more in panicky doubts. It was too soon, she couldn't do it, she was still at *school*, she didn't *know* enough, and now her parents might be in danger too. What happened if they weren't home? She paused, shaking, and called on the Badger's Gift of strength, as the Smith kicked the bike stand out. Then she ran past him and through the front door into the kitchen, shouting loudly. But there was no answer. The house was empty and silent. Merrilin and Nyneve Perry had not come back from Black Meadows.

The sound of the motorbike faded away as Linnet's feet stumbled back up the twisty stairs, jumping over the creaky step and knocking over spider plants as they went. She banged into her bedroom door and swore, rubbing her elbow as she went over to the chest where she had hidden her Gifts. There was no more time for lessons, and there could be no hiding, no more delays. The Maiden's real task started now, and she would have to do it as she was – unprepared and unready.

'Cloak,' she muttered, concentrating hard. 'Bottle, pouch.' She took a deep breath, squeezed her eyes tight shut, then opened them again to look round the comforting familiarity of her room. It all seemed so ordinary compared to what she was about to do. But her parents were in danger, and Petroc, and Zafira, not to mention Wyrmesbury and the whole world, she thought, slightly wildly. Then she saw, once again, Magret slipping off the wyrm's long talon, and clenched her fists, not looking away this time. It hardened her resolve like nothing else could have.

'Well,' she said to the walls. 'Looks like I'm the only one who can stop this thing. So I will.' And suddenly feeling quite brave and utterly determined to do what she had to, the Maiden put on Cernunnos's cloak and slipped unseen through the last rays of sunrise towards Hootcat Hill and the Door to Avvallon.

The Door to Avvallon

And see ye not yon bonny road
That winds about the fernie brae?
That is the Road to fair Elfland,
Where thou and I this night maun gae.

From 'The Ballad of Tam Linn the Rhymer'

Linnet fumbled the gesture of opening, and stumbled through the barrier into the centre of the Owlstones. The Beast Gladysant was curled around the largest stone, looking disgruntled, with a hootcat owl perched on her ear, and Mathafurd Llewellyn leaning against her back. The Owlman strode towards her, his bald head shining through the mist.

'The Door is ready to be opened, Linnet. Have you got everything you need?' Linnet looked at him and laughed. She couldn't help it. It was just so ridiculous – what did he mean 'need'? How could she know? Then the danger of her situation hit her once more, and she sobered up. The fact was that what she needed was within her, and she wouldn't know if it was enough until she used it.

'I'm probably the most unprepared Maiden in history,' she said. 'But I have my Guardian Gifts, if that's what you mean by need. And I'll have Mathafurd and Gladysant, too. Other than that, it's up to me.'

Gladysant howled mournfully as the hootcat pecked her feathery ear. Linnet hid a smile. It was hard to tell the hound voices apart, but she distinctly heard one moaning about disrespectful owls.

'You will be fine, Linnet,' said Professor Hullart gently. 'Your Powers as Maiden will protect you somewhat, but the awkward fact is that one minute in Avvallon is a day of mortal time.'

'But that means I'll never be back in time to put the wyrm back to sleep before it's destroyed everything,' said Linnet.

'Exactly,' said Mathafurd Llewellyn. 'So you need to think about making a spell. A new spell that only you can make. A spell that uses the old magic and the new technomagic, so that the Fey Folk will not be able to break it. The Queen is in the mortal world now, but only just, and it must be strong enough to prevent her coming back through and stopping you from doing what you must. You will have quite enough to do outwitting Fidget Reedglitter and the Prince.'

'Great,' said Linnet sarcastically. 'So now I get to be the saviour of the world *and* make up impossible new magic as well. Thanks for telling me. Not.' There was a waiting silence. Could she? she wondered. Could she really make a totally new kind of magic. If Mathafurd thought she could, it was probably possible. It was an exhilarating idea.

Maybe she wasn't so useless after all. She paced around the Owlstones, thinking furiously. How could she stop the Fey Queen and block the Door? A small *beep beep* sound broke the silence. Linnet pressed a button to switch off the alarm on her technowatch automatically. Then stopped. An idea had begun to form. She stared at her wrist, thinking so hard it felt as if her brain was creaking. Time. Time was the key to all this – or the lack of it. She had to give herself more. The small green digits on the technowatch blinked at her fluorescently, blindly marking . . . time.

There was a small click in her brain, as she suddenly realised what it was she had to do. Her Maiden memories chattered of the ancient art of spellmelding.

And that was it.

If she could meld mortal and Fey time into one matching whole for just a microsecond, she thought . . . if she could do that, it would give her enough force . . . to do what? she calculated frantically. Her brain whirred and ticked with so many difficult ideas that it felt as if it was about to burst.

Then it came. 'I can swing them round and swap them,' she muttered, new knowledge running through her in a hot, heady rush of Power. 'And if I use my technowatch as the key to hold the magic firm, the Fey will never break it – or not easily. It's going to be totally alien to them.'

Then she thought of something else. Something that stopped her thoughts and swung them in another direction entirely. Maybe, just maybe, she could save Magret. Quickly she took off the watch and reset the date and time to the previous week – just before Tom Bickerspike had disappeared. But then she paused. Now was not the right moment. Now she had another job to do.

'If this comes out right . . .' she said slowly, staring at it as she changed the watch back again to the present, 'I think I could eventually reverse time.' The Professor and Mathafurd gaped at her uncomprehendingly. No one had ever reversed time. It was impossible. Or it had been. Then Linnet continued. 'But for now I'm going to try and swap Fey and mortal time round. I'll use the technowatch to fix it so that it's unbreakable. Half an hour of mortal time should give me all the time I need in Avvallon. I'll have thirty days and nights and if I can't do it in that time then I won't be able to do it at all.' She looked at the Professor. 'Be ready to open the Door when I yell,' she said. 'And you be ready too, Mathafurd.'

'Be very careful, Maiden,' said the Professor. 'Are you sure you know what you are doing?'

'Of course I don't,' she snapped. 'I thought that was the whole point. No one has ever done this kind of spellmeld before me, at least my Maiden memories say they haven't – and no one's mixed magics either. But I'm going to try. There's no choice. If it doesn't work . . .' She shook her head, not wanting to think about that right now. She reached into her pouch and took out Fay's bottle of Airs, looking at it closely. This would have to be done right, and her Maiden memories told her that any spellmeld would be best done with an Air binding.

She muttered the wind seeking the harbours spell, and immediately the coloured streams of air whirled around her. She plucked colours at random, using instinct and Power together to make the spellmeld, muttering words torn out of the very heart of her being – words that made the air around her shiver and fragment. As the spellmeld started to take hold, she fought the drag and pull of the two times – Fey and mortal – each stretching her in so many directions that she screamed in pain. And then the moment came – a tiny window of perfect stillness where both times rested in one place. In a flash, Linnet bound the modern technomagic of her watch with the older enchantments and with a flick of her mind which made her cry out with pain once more, flipped the two times around. The air around the Owlstones fizzed and crackled with energy. Linnet held up the watch, now wreathed in a rainbow of coloured airs. Time stood bound to a technochip.

'Open the Door,' she said. And her voice sounded slow and deep and treacly and very far away. The earth began to shake.

'What have you done?' cried the Professor, as he felt the spellmeld affect his very bones. Mathafurd seized his arm and shook it, before scrambling onto Gladysant.

'Open the Door,' he cried. 'Or it will be too late. The wyrm moves again!'

The Professor took his owl-headed staff and struck the earth before the biggest Owlstone once.

> '*Troimh thir eadar Aisling!*
> *Through a Land without Dreams!*'

he cried in a loud voice.

And as he did so, an open door appeared in the stone, golden mist hiding what lay beyond. Linnet grabbed

Mathafurd's hand, leapt onto Gladysant's back and flung her technowatch at the entrance.

'Cùm air ais tìm!
Hold back Time!'

She yelled the command of Power out as she moved, and the technowatch caught and hung in the centre of the Door, revolving slowly as the final part of the spellmeld was set in motion. There was a perceptible jolt as the new magic took effect. Then the mist changed to copper, and Linnet, Mathafurd and Gladysant disappeared through the Door to Avvallon, together with one very surprised hootcat owl. The Door sealed itself behind them with a clash. Faster than the eye could see, it grew a thicket of steely thorns around itself. Each had a green, fluorescent tip that glowed and blinked.

Professor Hullart felt his skull. There was a large bump where he had struck the owlstone as the backlash of Linnet's magic had caught him and flung him to the ground. As he struggled back to his feet, Cernunnos galloped into the circle.

'What has she done?' he roared.

The Professor shook his head gingerly. 'Changed Time,' he said. 'I think. But the Door is closed to all – Fey and mortal – until she returns and reverses the spell.'

'But I am neither Fey nor Mortal,' said Cernunnos. 'And I have other ways in, as none of the rest of you do. I shall go and keep a hidden eye on what she is doing, without interfering unless I must.' He shook his horned head angrily. '*Why* must it always be an untrained Maiden, without the rest of us? The Fey will be very angry at what she has done.'

'I know,' said Professor Hullart gloomily. 'I think the Queen would probably kill Linnet if she had the strength. Her anti-ageing spells will all have fallen into ruin if this spell does what I think it does, and Avvallon itself will be in danger. If Linnet does not hurry, the Queen may be irretrievably weakened beyond the repair of even Fidget Reedglitter's sorceries, and Avvallon . . . I do not know about Avvallon.' The earth shook once more. 'And feel, the wyrm moves once more and we shall have to manage to contain it until the Maiden returns. I do not think the Fey will help us now.'

'If Linnet returns at all,' said Cernunnos, his voice grim. Professor Hullart turned away from him and began to send out an urgent Need Call to the other Guardians. He had faith in Linnet, even if Cernunnos did not. The alternative was too horrible to contemplate.

The motorbike seemed to freeze in mid roar as Time changed and slowed around it. 'She's through,' said Wayland over his shoulder to Petroc. 'Whatever she's done, she's through.' Then he saw Merrilin Perry's car, parked by Black Meadows. It was torn in half, empty and forlorn. Merrilin and Nyneve were nowhere to be seen, and the earth was shaking.

Linnet, Mathafurd and Gladysant landed with a bump, rolling over and over in a tangle of wings and legs and fur. The hootcat screeched shrilly as one of Gladysant's hooves clipped him on the tail. Linnet disentangled herself and stood up, so excited and so scared that her whole body tingled with it. She'd done it! This was really, truly Avvallon and she was actually in another world! She took a deep breath of the pure, cold air that smelled somehow alien and familiar at the same time. She could feel her heart beating strong and sure in her chest, but it felt slower, denser than normal, as if her life was on pause. Which it was here, she supposed, given that she'd stretched time with her spellmeld. She somehow didn't feel like the old Linnet Perry anymore, but she didn't know why yet. She only knew that now the edges of what made her herself felt stretched and changed, and the Linnet who stood in Avvallon was subtly different to the Linnet who lived in Wyrmesbury. Perhaps I'm just more magical here, she thought, as she gazed out on a world where the air glittered strangely, as if behind a transparent silver veil.

Linnet noticed that the purple hills seemed to have a quality that was indefinably more hilly than her own mortal world, the grass was a greener green, the bracken and scrub a more intense brown and the landscape shifted and changed endlessly, scrolling from spring to summer and back through summer again. Small drooping blue harebells bloomed alongside bright celandine and clumps of drifting purple willow herb in a mad floral muddle. There was absolutely nothing living to be seen – not Fey nor animal, bird or insect – and it was totally silent, apart from the rumbling, complaining hound voices in Gladysant's belly.

She shook herself out of her reverie as the hootcat landed on her shoulder, still screeching its complaints against Gladysant. She stroked it absently, soothing its ruffled feathers.

'Now what?' she asked. 'Where do we start looking for Fidget Reedglitter and this Chalice of Athyr? Because I have no idea at all. You're the one who's been here before.' Mathafurd climbed down from Gladysant's back and looked around him, scratching his beard thoughtfully.

'Yes, I have been here before – many times to visit my kin as well as with other Maidens. But it changes every time. Although it looks empty there are always unfriendly eyes about, and we will need to stay hidden. The Fey Folk and their creatures will soon be watching for you. They do not like to age even by a day, and the time magic you did will soon affect the Queen,' said Mathafurd. 'Not to mention that it is time for the Changeover, and the Queen is now trapped in the mortal world. The Prince will certainly notice when he and his guards cannot get through those thorns round the Door.

'But others live in Avvallon as well as the Fey Folk. Others who hate the Fey and will aid us if it will thwart them in any way. I think we must go and find my cousin Gilla Filiflower, who is one of the Huldafolk, who are the hidden people of the Rowan. They know most things that happen here in Avvallon. And what they don't know they can find out.' Mathafurd grimaced. 'My great-grandfather on my mother's side was a Hulda – it's why I have these blasted pointy ears that make me look like some kind of short elf – and that means I can claim bloodkin right from them.'

'What's that?' Linnet asked, curious.

Mathafurd grinned nastily through his beard. 'It

basically means that Gilla must grant me one favour because we're related. She's a grumpy sort, and she won't like it, but she knows the bloodkin rules as well as I do.'

'It's sort of like collecting a debt, then?'

'Yes, that's as good a way of looking at it as any. I'll be collecting a debt for all the teasing I've had about my Hulda ears from the other dwarves! Still, perhaps it was worth it if it means I can be of service to the Maiden.'

'Right,' said Linnet, suppressing the familiar wave of guilt that washed over her every time she remembered how much the Maiden was disrupting Mathafurd's life. 'You're the guide. Let's go and meet these pointy-eared cousins of yours. I've got a bad feeling about staying near this Door for too long. I think those unfriendly eyes are not far off.'

The hootcat owl shrieked its agreement into her ear, as far away a small, lime-green cloud hung lazily in the sky.

chapter eleven

Woodcock and Rowanberry

Red rowanberries to keep her from harm . . .
For Fey have no power 'gainst a Witchen-tree charm . . .

From 'Eolin's Herbal for Seers'

Gladysant's pink wings folded as she glided to earth at the edge of a large forest glade of rowan trees. Linnet noticed once again the strange mixing of seasons that seemed to exist here. Weirdly, some of the trees were laden with huge, sweet smelling creamy blossoms, while others drooped with bunches of bright red-orange berries.

'The Hulda live near wherever rowan trees bloom,' said Mathafurd. 'And they miss nothing that happens in their domain.' He cleared his throat. 'Ho!' he called softly. 'Ho! Gilla Filiflower. Are you sleeping? Bloodkin calls to bloodkin.' The trees rustled and swayed in the never-ending soft breeze, but there was no answer.

'Looks like your cousin will only be found if she wants to be,' said Linnet, after Mathafurd had called several times more.

'I think it's best if I go and look for her, Linnet. You and Gladysant must stay hidden here where it's safe. The Fey won't enter a rowan grove willingly – the trees have some sort of warding magic against them. So while you are waiting for me to come back, thread yourself a necklace of rowanberries. It may come in useful later on. I will send a messenger to fetch you when I've found Gilla. She usually has some sort of bird hanging round her.' Then he disappeared behind the silvery trunks with not a rustle, even through the ground was covered with fallen leaves.

Linnet eyed Gladysant. The hootcat owl was still clinging tightly to one ear – a pathetic, huddled ball of feathers with tightly closed eyes.

'Just us, then,' she said, still finding it strange to be talking to what she supposed was a mythical beast. Gladysant stared back with golden, eagle eyes and clacked her enormous beak disdainfully.

'Our wings hurt,' rumbled a hound voice from the vicinity of her belly.

'Yes,' growled several others. 'And we're hungry.'

There was a slight pause. 'Very hungry.'

The long dragon tail swished menacingly, and Linnet took a step back. Then she stepped forward again, hands on hips. This was ridiculous, she had a job to do, and this oversized monster was not going to ruin it before she even began.

'You,' she said firmly, 'are never ever to even think about eating ME. I am the Maiden, and I would not taste at all nice. Added to which I know lots of spells which would give you really bad indigestion for a year, and I don't think you'd like that. So shut up and pick me some berries. I can't reach.' There was some discontented whining, but Gladysant reached up her beak and snipped a bunch of berries, which she dropped at Linnet's feet. Then she turned her back, folded her eight legs under her, curled up and seemingly went to sleep. The hootcat did the same. Linnet picked a long, strong strand of grass and a sharp thorn, and sat down with her back against a tree. Absorbed in her necklace threading, she failed to notice a bright, black eye watching her from behind a bush.

'Ahem,' said a quiet voice. She looked up. There in front of her stood a stocky, mottled brown bird with a long beak. It looked quite ordinary and innocent, but she challenged it anyway. Better to be safe than sorry, said the Maiden voices in her head.

'Who are you?' she asked. 'What do you want?'

'I am Woodcock,' said the bird. 'The harper sent me.'

'How do I know you're not some Fey trick?'

'The dwarf told me to say that he met you in a kitchen, if you were to doubt me.'

'All right,' said Linnet. 'I suppose nobody else would know that. What do you want me to do?'

Woodcock peered out of the edge of the grove. A small, angry dark green cloud was heading in their direction, moving fast. He shook his feathers distractedly. It was a bad sign and they must hurry. 'Come with me quickly now, I will take you to Mathafurd and my mistress.' Gathering her berry necklace into her pouch, Linnet told Gladysant and the hootcat to stay where they were, and followed the bird into the forest. The paths changed and shifted under her feet and it seemed to her that the trees were talking secrets. But the Owlman's Gift was only for the language of creatures, and it did not allow her to understand them.

At last they came to a huge mossy cliff, with a waterfall sliding down it into a still pool. At the edge of the pool stood Mathafurd and a small, round person with long purple ears which twitched slightly at the points. Linnet smiled to herself. The ears were, indeed, a larger, pointier, more colourful version of Mathafurd's. She was wearing a cloak of feathers which looked alarmingly like those of Linnet's guide, and rowanberries dangled from her oversized earlobes.

'But she's just a girl,' the person muttered to herself irritably. 'What can just a girl do against the likes of Fidget Reedglitter and the Fey Queen? Ridiculous.' She snorted and turned as if to walk away, but Mathafurd caught her by the arm.

'This is the Maiden, Linnet Perry,' he said sternly. 'She is strong in the Power – and she has made a new kind of magic that has never been seen before today. Anyway, my *bloodkin* cousin,' he added in a meaningful voice, 'I am sworn to see this task through, and so are you, if you remember our little conversation of five minutes ago.'

'Oh, very well. If you will insist on this bloodkin oath nonsense,' she said, her voice testy as she turned back to face Linnet. 'I am Gilla Filiflower, and this is the Rowan Rath – home of the Huldafolk. You'd better come in through the back.' And with that she turned and waded into the pool, lifting her skirts to reveal stout, purple legs with large, webbed feet at the ends. As Linnet and Mathafurd followed, Woodcock flew up into the air, drifting back into the trees on silent wings.

Shaking the water from her hair and eyes, Linnet looked around her. She was in a large room with a blazing purple fire in the centre. Several Huldafolk were bustling about, weaving in and out of the pillars that dotted the room. She noticed that they were carved into perfect replicas of rowan trees, blossom, berries and all, and that they appeared to be made of a kind of crystal which gave off a soft glow which lit the room.

'Sit here, both of you, and mind you keep quiet,' said Gilla, pointing to stools by one of the pillars. 'We will need the Wiser Branch and the Singer for this.' She stumped off, muttering again.

'Is she usually this friendly,' asked Linnet sarcastically, 'or is it just me? And what are the Wiser Branch and the Singer when they're at home?' Mathafurd grinned ruefully. This Maiden did seem to ask a lot of questions. But he supposed he'd signed up for the job of looking after her, and maybe answering her myriad questions was a part of that . . .

He began to explain. 'The People of the Rowan are well-known for three things: the wisdom of trees; the music of water – and the grumpiness of crones. They have three leaders, the Wiser Branch and the Singer, whom Gilla has gone to fetch. Gilla herself is the third – and her title is the Gruff. She is there to be the balance, the cautionary voice, the guard against recklessness. It is she who has kept them hidden and prevented them from being tangled in the wiles of the Fey. She may be a little cantankerous, but her heart is good. And if anyone knows how to outwit Fidget Reedglitter, it is her.' As he finished speaking, Gilla returned with two figures identical to herself except that one had a cloak of green leaves and the other a cloak of what looked like woven dandelion fluff.

'This,' she announced, pointing at Linnet, 'is the mortal Maiden. She brings trouble, nothing but trouble, but there's no help for it, I have been bamboozled into a bloodkin promise by my dwarf cousin here, curse his harper's silver tongue, so we shall have to give her aid.' Green Cloak laughed.

'Always the voice of doom, Gilla the Gruff,' she said. 'Welcome, Maiden. I am the Wiser Branch of this Rath and this is our Singer. Tell us your need, and we will do what we can.'

Linnet felt a bit awkward and shy suddenly. Her natural inclination was to hide and try to avoid being noticed – that was what she did at school after all. Being at the centre of things had not been a good experience for her in the past. But this was different. Right now she was actually the focus of some positive attention, it seemed. She found it slightly unnerving, but the smiles of the Singer and the Wiser Branch encouraged her to begin her tale. She cleared her throat.

'Well,' she started slowly, 'there's this big wyrm thing . . .' There was a long silence after she had finished her story, then the Wiser Branch sighed.

'Gilla is right, you are trouble. Or at least you bring it. Why is it that mortals are always meddling in things best left alone? That greedy boy—' she broke off, then squared her shoulders. 'But what is done is done. We will all suffer if the worldwyrm is not put back into his deepest sleep again. And I suspect we may also suffer if your new technomagic has crept from the mortal world into the rest of Avvallon. I must check the Spells of Hiding to make sure they have not been affected. We do not want the Fey to find us – especially now that you are here.'

'Yes,' said the Singer. 'The Fey Prince went out from Caer Criostal this morning. He will be well on his way to the Door by now. And when he finds it bespelled and shut, he will smell that there is trouble. He will most likely send his huntsman and their Hounds out to chase down whoever has done this – there is no doubt that the Hounds will smell that someone has come through – or the Prince himself. He has a fine nose for magic, they say.'

'So what do I do?' asked Linnet. This was getting all too real and scary. She didn't like the sound of hounds chasing her down one bit. But she fought her fears and asked the question she most wanted an answer to. 'How do I find where Fidget Reedglitter has hidden the Chalice of Athyr and the elixir? And how do I steal it without being noticed?'

'The sorceress was seen near the ocean, several days before she summoned the mortal music girl,' said Gilla. 'The seagulls brought me word.'

Linnet's heart gave a great thump. She had totally forgotten about Zafira.

'Oh, no!' she said. Mathafurd and the three Hulda looked at her enquiringly.

'I shall have to rescue the person you call the mortal

music girl as well as everything else. Her name is Zafira and she's my best friend's sister. I can't just leave her here – Petroc would kill me.' She groaned. How could she possibly do everything in time? Thirty days and nights had seemed plenty, but now she wasn't so sure. How much time had passed already since she had worked her technomagic spell? She realised with a shock that she didn't really know. It was so hard to keep track of time here – it seemed slipperier and more fluid than mortal time, which divided up into useful segments of seconds and minutes and hours. She rubbed her wrist absently, missing the feel of her watch. How long was she going to have to spend in this cave, she thought impatiently? She cleared her throat to ask. But then the three Hulda finished their whispering to each other and looked up.

'We will go and check the Spells, and see if we can discover more about what Fidget was doing by the ocean. There is food to be had, and rest. We will come and find you in the morning.' They left, and disappeared behind the rowan pillars. Linnet thumped the bench in frustration. Her unspoken question was answered – and very unsatisfactorily too. At least a night here, then, before she could get on and do what she was meant to.

Mathafurd stood up and stretched. 'I shall go and get us something to eat. You stay here and finish that necklace.'

'What's so important about the wretched necklace? It's only some old berries on grass.' Linnet asked crossly. She could at least get a proper answer about that, she thought.

But it seemed not. 'You'll see soon enough,' said Mathafurd mysteriously. And he strolled off in the direction of a cauldron which bubbled and simmered on the purple fire, emitting delicious smells of mushroom and something else which Linnet couldn't quite place.

'Annoying dwarf,' she grumbled, getting the berries out of her pouch and beginning to work on them again. There was nothing else to do, and at least the mindless work of pierce and thread, pierce and thread was soothing to her brain and fingers.

After a rather silent supper, she wrapped Cernunnos's cloak tightly around her, falling asleep to the strains of Mathafurd's harp and the sound of his voice singing a song of the Huldafolk in a language she didn't know but understood all the same. Her belly was pleasantly overfull with mushroom, but she still didn't know what else had been in the stew.

Linnet had a restless night. Her sleeping was full of things and people and places which she knew enough by now to realise, even as she tossed and turned, were true and important to her quest. But in that annoyingly slippery way of dreams, she couldn't capture any vision long enough to really hold onto it. In quick and confusing succession, she saw monsters of the deep bound in torment – one a vast white whale, one huge and serpentlike; crowds of merrfolk crying and searching the ocean for something; a room full of withered leaves in a crystal palace; a deep pool with something nameless and horrible in its depths. The very last dream was of a small, menacing dark green cloud that chased her down, smothering her in its amorphous, damp embrace until she couldn't breathe. She awoke, stifling, under a pile of thistledown blankets with a hand shaking her shoulder.

It was Gilla the Gruff. 'Wake up, sleepyhead,' she said in her usual cross manner. 'Things look bad, and likely to get worse. Come with me. You've missed out on breakfast, of course, but that's your problem, not mine.'

Linnet didn't bother to reply. There seemed no point in encouraging more of Gilla's grumpiness. So she just rubbed the sleep out of her eyes and shrugged the kinks out of her shoulders (the floor had been very hard). She wasn't hungry anyway, after last night's filling supper. She followed Gilla out of the pillar room, pondering her dreams, and trying to ignore the complaints and mutterings in front of her. Her Maiden voices were yattering in her head. Pay attention to the merr! they said, and Linnet knew they were right. So as Gilla led her along a series of interconnecting passages, she filed all the images away into her memory for mulling over when she had more time. Like that's going to be soon, she thought to herself. But the deepest part of herself suddenly became aware that there was definitely something important she needed to remember. Something about the merrfolk's searching that rang a bell, not in her Maiden life, but in the life before. BM, she said to herself, smiling at the fleeting thought. Before Maiden. Then she remembered where she was and what she had to do AM. After Maiden. That didn't seem quite so funny.

At last they came out into a perfectly round, domed space which shone with a green light like sunshine on spring leaves. Mathafurd was already there, as were the Wiser Branch and the Singer, all staring into a wide, shallow stone bowl that floated at waist height from the floor. Mathafurd, being even shorter than the Hulda, was peering over the edge with some difficulty.

Linnet stepped forward. The picture in the bowl was much like the one she had Seen in the Feyglass. An ancient Fey, who she recognised as Fidget Reedglitter, stood out in the middle of a bay, waves lapping round her ankles. She appeared to be standing on the sea itself. Gilla blew softly on the picture, and then they could all hear as well as See.

'Muc Mara,' cried Fidget Reedglitter. 'Muc Mara the White! I summon you in the name of the Oak Leaf, in the name of the filly that was never foaled, and in the name of the drowned souls who sing under the waves of Lir.' All at once there was a commotion, and a huge white head rose from the sea, opening a vast mouth full of pointed teeth. A great waft of ancient, rotted fish, and other unmentionable things came out of the bowl. It appeared that not only could they hear and See, but they could smell too. Linnet put her hand to her mouth, gagging and amazed at the same time. The white whale was one of the monsters from her dream. 'Hush,' said Gilla, staring at Linnet sternly. Linnet breathed in carefully through her mouth and looked back at the bowl silently.

Fidget Reedglitter put out her hands to steady herself on the jawbones of the great whale, and climbed into the mouth, standing unsteadily on the tongue and then walking down the throat, where she disappeared from view for a moment, before reappearing, clutching a golden cup. It was, as far as the watchers could see, empty.

The picture faded, and the bowl cleared. 'Is that the Chalice of Athyr?' Linnet asked, though she knew perfectly well it was. The Maiden voices were telling her so. Not waiting for an answer she carried on. 'Just as well I didn't have to get it from in there. I don't think I could have stood the smell.'

The small joke fell into a flat silence, as the Wiser Branch looked at her. 'You may have to go into worse places than that. Fidget is not known for her pleasant habits. Now, we must look for a clue to where the elixir is – if she has finished making it. The dragonwort grows in only one place now, and it is very scarce and hard to find. Fidget may keep the Chalice near her now she's retrieved it, probably in her rooms at Caer Criostal, or she may not. But we know of old that she will keep it away from the elixir. That will be in a different place entirely. The Power of the two must not be mixed until the moment the Fey Queen returns. And of course, we know now that that is not going to happen because you have closed the Door against her.'

Gilla blew on the bowl again, and this time a different picture appeared.

Fidget Reedglitter was pounding a small piece of bloodred root, and scraping the results into a bubbling pot from which bright yellow steam rose. As she did so, the steam changed to the deep blue-purple of a midnight sky and she reached out behind her and seized what looked like a long, shiny black bag.

'Open up,' she cackled. 'Open up, my pretty big belly, my Bru Mhor. It is done.' The bag opened its jaws. It was a massive leech. She poured the boiling liquid straight into the waiting mouth, with no apparent ill-effects to the leech. It merely swelled and swelled until it reached gargantuan proportions. Slime dripped from its sides.

'Close now, Bru Mhor,' said the Fey sorceress. She took a bone needle from her pocket and sewed the leech's mouth shut. Then she took it outside and dropped it into a pool full of green, viscous mud, where it sank to the bottom and disappeared. Once again, a waft of rottenness blew out of the bowl. The picture faded, but not before they had seen Fidget muttering the words of a spell over the pool.

'Ugh,' said Linnet. 'Ugh! That poor leech. I mean, I know they're not very nice things . . . but still, sewing it up like that. And that smell. I'm going to have to go in there, aren't I? And pick up that leech,' she continued in a rather sick-sounding voice. 'And carry it home with me.'

'I told you Fidget was none too nice in her habits,' said the Wiser Branch.

'That,' said Linnet, shuddering, 'is the understatement of the century. She's like, totally evil. She's the wicked witch in all the stories Dad used to tell me when I was a little kid. But she's real. Isn't she?'

The Singer looked at her compassionately, her dandelion fluff cloak catching the light and turning to golden softness.

'Yes, Linnet. She is.'

chapter twelve

Maiden and Prince

A handsome Prince came riding by
Hillo hillo lillo li
Towards the Doorway he would go
But Doors may shut and Princes die
Chall o ro hi ho

From 'Father Gander's Nursery Rhymes'

The Fey Prince strode out in front, followed by a host of Fey Folk. His green skin shone in the sunshine, and at his side a minstrel played a new tune – one that he had learnt from the mortal girl who had been Summoned by Fidget. The music made the Prince uneasy. Everything felt faster than normal and somehow unnatural, but he couldn't put his finger on what it was. And he was never happy about going into the mortal world. He didn't like putting off his nice solid green Avvallon body (which he was rather proud of) and becoming insubstantial and wispy as all Fey did in the mortal world. And guarding the wyrm was so boring. It had only been a joke, leading that inquisitive mortal girl down to its lair. They had never thought it would lead to such a harsh punishment for so long, nor such a diminution of their Powers.

Surely, he thought, as he always did at this moment, there must be some way to get out of it. Some new spell they could use to bind it forever in sleep, even if it meant working with that Maiden the mortals produced every time one of their greedy race woke it up with their diggings and delvings. Then he and the Queen could be together again as they had not for millennia of mortal time. The parties and banquets were not the same without her, and even when the fabled White Hart appeared (which was almost never, these days), the hunt was not as much fun unless she was at his side. He sighed. The Queen hated Maidens almost as much as Fidget did. He'd never get them to work with a mortal – Avvallon itself would have to be at stake before they did that, and Avvallon was invincible while the Queen ruled. He raised his head. They were approaching the Door. It was time for the Changeover.

'Prepare yourselves to welcome your Queen,' he cried, the words of Opening hovering on his lips.

But what was this? The Door was wreathed in metal thorns and coppery mist. How had this happened? He sniffed the air. There was a smell of mortal – and something else. Dwarf, he thought, with a whiff of . . . what? He shrugged – the Queen would be waiting, she could deal with it on her return.

'*Fosgail an doras basmhor!*' he commanded in the time-honoured way, but nothing happened. The Prince said the words of Opening more loudly. Again and again he commanded the Door to the mortal world to open. Finally he threw himself at it, screaming the spell over and over and beating at it with his fists. The metal thorns stabbed at him, and a rush of strange magic, the like of which he had never felt before took him, and flung him at the Door, so that he hung there, spreadeagled and flattened like a leaf against it.

'Find whoever has done this,' he croaked to his chief huntsman, as Avvallon faded before his eyes. 'Look for a mortal and a dwarf and another thing – a beast or a bird. Find them and imprison them till I can deal with them. But not before you have forced them to undo what they have wrought here. The Queen must return. Avvallon itself is in danger!' Then his head slumped and the copper mist covered him and hid him from sight. There was a loud, satisfied ticking sound, then silence.

One by one, the ugly, raw-boned white Yelp hounds lifted their heads and howled their anguish and terror at their Prince's disappearance. The tall, thin Fey huntsman moved among them, whispering and comforting, and as they calmed, they milled round him aimlessly, waiting for his command. The courtiers too, milled and moped like a crowd of lost deer, too shocked to speak. He looked at the copper mist, still hanging in front of the Door. Never before had he been put in command like this – but he must obey the Prince's last order.

'Ho!' he said, summoning a page with one long finger. 'Run for Caer Criostal as quick as you can, and tell the sorceress that she must delay the feast. Tell her what has happened here.'

'But . . . but what of the Queen?' stammered the page over his shoulder as he set off. His words hung in the air behind him like leaden raindrops.

'Yes, yes, what of the Queen?' muttered the Fey Folk. 'And what did the Prince mean by "Avvallon is in danger"?'

Bombus Bentsap, the Lord Chamberlain stepped forward. 'If the Queen does not drink the elixir from the Chalice, then she will age by uncountable centuries . . .' His voice dropped, as the unthinkable words spilled out. 'The Fey can only have a Queen who is young and beautiful. That is what our Prince meant. The Queen is tied to Avvallon. If she ages, so does the land. We will be living in a dry, dead wilderness if the Changeover Ceremony does not take place . . .' Once more, the hounds howled. Animal and Fey both knew in their very bones that disaster loomed if the Queen was shut out of her own country.

'To the chase,' yelled the huntsman, setting his hounds to pick up the scent.

'To the chase,' cried the Fey host, as the hounds started to give tongue. But they could not follow a scent in the air.

The page cringed away as Fidget Reedglitter cursed. She threw a holding spell over the preparations for the Queen's Homecoming banquet. Everything was ready, and now this absurd message had come. She did not understand it at all. The Door had never remained closed before. And as for the news that the Prince had disappeared – that was obviously nonsense. The Fey did not disappear in their own lands. That incompetent huntsman must have got it wrong, but she would have to go and see for herself.

For the first time in her ages-long life she felt a pang of doubt. The Chalice was in its new hiding place, awaiting the Queen's return. Should she take it with her? No, she decided. It would be safer here, scattered as it was. The danger was obviously elsewhere. No one could possibly reassemble it, and if they did, her spell of protection would catch them. She cast a hurried, careless closing magic at her door, and went down to the courtyard, where there was a loud and panicky hustle of kitchenhands and servants.

'Sheep!' she said contemptuously, pushing her way through them as they streamed out of the gates to join the hunt. She cursed again. How had she not seen this coming? Her watchcloud was in the sky above, and should have warned her of any strangers entering Avvallon. But it was a lazy thing, and always half asleep. She sent out a bolt of angry magic towards it, and felt it start guiltily, wake up and change colour from lime to dark green as it sped across the sky. Her vision locked onto it, and she saw, in her cloud's eye view, the land spread out in its ever-changing beauty. There was no movement except for the hunt. But the cloud would miss nothing from now on, or she would turn it into acid rain to use in her potions. Coming back to earth, she summoned her young airdragon with a piercing whistle. Others might run, but Fidget Reedglitter would ride the wind. And if the news was true, then someone would pay. She licked her lips. She would take great pleasure in that.

*

Linnet was fed up. They had been arguing and talking about the best way to go for so long that she didn't think she could hear another word without screaming. Why did grown-ups always have to make things so complicated? If she had to do this, she just wanted to get on with it. Now. But first the Singer had yattered away some more about Fidget Reedglitter's nastiness, and how careful she would have to be to avoid running into her (like Linnet didn't already get that), then the Wiser Branch had been all practical about geography and magicked out some maps from a hidden cupboard. Then Grumpy Gilla had whinged on and on and on about how she didn't want to do this (with many asides about wretched dwarves who thought they were owed something, and useless Maidens who would probably fail when it came down to the crunch, so she'd better go along to see that the business was done properly). Linnet gave up arguing in the end. Mathafurd seemed to be doing a good job of fighting her corner for her, so she let the discussion drift past her (while seeming to concentrate, just like she did with Mum and Dad sometimes) and thought about merrfolk. Whatever it was she needed to know continued to elude her, so she left it once more, since, finally, to her relief, a conclusion seemed to have been reached at last on what she should do next.

'So,' said Gilla. 'It is decided. I will guide you to Caer Criostal by the secret ways to try and find the Chalice. Once you have that you will be in a better position to go on and find the elixir. The Chalice is a powerful object in itself and you will be able to use it to protect yourself from Fidget. Meanwhile, Mathafurd will retrieve his Beast, and lay a false trail in case the Prince and his hounds discover you are in Avvallon. Which they undoubtedly will as soon as they reach that Door and smell your footprints round it,' she finished gloomily.

Linnet wasn't thrilled about having Grumpy Gilla as her guide. But Mathafurd had promised to join her as soon as he could, and to send the hootcat to her with messages if there was a delay. She supposed that would have to do. And it was a relief to be really getting on with it at last. She was very aware that her thirty days and nights could disappear all too quickly here, despite the technowatch spell.

Having said their goodbyes to Mathafurd, the Wiser Branch and the Singer, they set off, Gilla carrying a bag of supplies and a stout stick made of knotted rowan.

'Tread soft, and follow my footsteps,' she said over her shoulder. 'And try not to make too much noise. Mortals always make too much noise.'

Linnet sighed. She could see it was going to be a long journey. As they stepped out of the pool and into the forest, the Woodcock flew down and settled on Linnet's shoulder.

'News,' he said. 'The Door has worked a strange magic on the Fey Prince and he has disappeared. His hounds are out now with the rest of the Fey Folk, hunting for the Maiden and the dwarf, with orders to imprison them if found. And Fidget's search cloud is in the sky. It's green-black and angry, and it's looking for them too.'

Linnet shivered. She'd dreamed about that cloud, and she didn't want to come across it for real. She had a nasty feeling it might suffocate her properly next time she encountered it.

'Ha!' snorted Gilla. 'I knew it. Trouble. Nothing but trouble. We shall have to go down by the tunnels to the Halls of Annuvin. It is a long way, but there is a stream there leading to Caer Criostal, and we can get in from underneath.' Gilla muttered on under her breath about the inconvenience, and mortal meddling.

'Thank you,' whispered Linnet to the bird, stroking his soft feathers, as he opened his wings to fly away. But her heart had started to pound with fear. What would the Fey huntsmen do to her if they caught her, let alone that wretched sorceress's green cloud? And what kind of hounds were they? Would they eat her? Could she fight them off with her Power? She fumbled in her pouch for the bottle of Airs and started thinking of spells, running them over and over in her mind so that she would be ready. Anything was better than listening to Gilla's incessant mumbled predictions of disaster.

She was so busy with her thoughts that when Gilla suddenly ducked down into what looked like a mess of tree roots, she almost failed to notice, and had to swerve noisily, earning a 'tssk!' of annoyance from her guide. There was a tunnel between the roots, leading into the earth. It was dark and dank with mould and brackets of oddly shaped fungi which glowed with an unhealthy light. Linnet had to bend low to walk in it at all, and soon her back and knees were aching from the strain.

'I feel like Alys,' she thought. 'Chasing after that stupid White Rabbit. Now all it needs is the Fey Queen to order my head chopped off.'

Linnet was soon gritting her teeth and hating the sight of Gilla's small, straight back as they crept slowly on and on.

The Hulda woman, of course, did not have to bend at all, being so short, and her whispered remarks about clumsy mortals every time Linnet banged her head on a protruding root were really beginning to get on the one nerve she had left. To block her out, Linnet tried to remember the twists and turns to right and left with the part of her mind that wasn't practicing spells, but it was impossible. There were just too many, and quite quickly she didn't even know whether she was going backwards or forwards anymore.

The journey fell into a dull thing to be got through simply by putting one weary foot in front of another in the faint and unearthly fungi-light that changed from green to an unattractive kind of khaki-yellow as they progressed. She had chanted every protection, defence and attack spell she knew over and over hundreds of times in her head by the time the passage eventually grew taller. It seemed like a billion years since she had last stood upright, and it was bliss to her cramped and aching back and limbs as she stopped and stretched. But the feeling of relief did not last for long. After an all too brief rest, Grumpy Gilla urged her on again. The passages were straighter this time, but the air grew steadily damper and more foul smelling, till Linnet was trying not to choke and breathing in only through her mouth. The foulness came to a head just as they passed through an arch of tree roots into an enormous cavern, dully lit by more fungus, where a stream chattered and tinkled merrily across the centre.

At the very moment they set foot in the water, a huge voice roared, 'Harrrh! Got you, Mortal!' Linnet felt a large clammy something clamp on the back of her neck. It reeked of old, festering flesh and rotten things long decayed under the earth.

Linnet stifled a scream of pent-up rage, whirling round as she drew out a strand of red Earth Power and threw it with all her strength, muttering one of her well-prepared attack spells as she did so. The creature let go of her with a grunt, and thumped into the stream with a splash, totally entangled in sticky ropes of creeper. It was hairy and huge, with pointed, dirty fangs. The smell of it was unbelievably vile, which was unsurprising, since it was covered in green slimy weed from its waist down to its hooves, and it had what looked like mouldy, green bones in its raggedy, tangled facial hair. She stepped back, wrinkling her nose in digust. When she got home – if she got home – she was going to take care never to go near anything bad smelling ever again.

'Ah,' said Gilla coming to stand beside Linnet. 'The Affank of Annuvin. It enslaves mortals when it can get them, makes them scrub its pots and brush its hair. And I don't think this one has had a slave for a long time by the looks of him. Well, perhaps you are not so useless after all. I see you can defend yourself at a pinch.'

'Yes,' said Linnet. 'I can. So less of the grumbling, please.' She turned to the beast. 'As for you,' she said, glaring at it. 'I don't like being sneaked up on from behind. It makes me a bit cross, see?' The Affank nodded as well as it could through the ropes. It wasn't so brave now. 'What shall I do with it?' she asked Gilla.

Gilla smirked nastily. It was the first time Linnet had seen her smile, and immediately she could see the resemblance to Mathafurd. It was something about the way the ears moved with the grin. 'If you let it go, it will owe you a life,' she said. 'That's a big debt in Avvallon. It won't like it at all, but it will have to do what you say until the debt is paid.'

'Right,' said Linnet. 'I'll untie you,' she said to the Affank. 'But you have to help us find Fidget Reedglitter's rooms. Then we'll see. I think I might send you to go out and keep the Prince's hounds off our trail. Or I might consider letting you off — eventually. Oh, and you can't tell anyone I'm here.' The Affank nodded its agreement miserably, so Linnet gestured, and the ropes spun into a thread of red Air and rushed back into the open bottle.

'Affank doesn't like hounds,' it wheezed miserably. 'They taste bad.'

'Tough,' said Linnet, turning to follow Gilla again. 'Use a mouthwash. And find some deodorant while you're at it.'

The Affank's small brain gave up. Whatever the mouthwash deodorant thing was, it must be very strong magic, and the Affank didn't have it. Or want to.

The bony white hounds lolloped over the ever-changing landscape, quartering back and forth, their huge red ears twitching and pricking. They had been running for uncounted time, with the Fey Folk behind them, but they were not tired yet, even though they had found no trace of the scent from the Door. Then the lead hound picked up a trace of something and stopped, bewildered. There was a hint of the human and a stronger touch of dwarf stink, but mostly it was like nothing he had ever smelt before. It was a mixture of dragon and deer and eagle and owl and . . . he sniffed again suspiciously... hounds. A red mist came over his eyes. Other hounds. Rivals. In his pack's territory. He lifted his head and bayed for the others to follow, running swiftly towards the distant mountains, well away from Caer Criostal.

Lying hidden behind a boulder, Mathafurd watched with satisfaction. The long hours spent laying down false tracks which led nowhere had obviously paid off. He turned to the Beast, now resting as a tattoo on his arm again. 'Well done, Gladysant, my dear. Fooled them. They should follow that for a very long time. Let's hope it throws them off the real trail entirely. Now we can get back to Linnet.' The tattoo wriggled in a gratified way. The hootcat, which was now sitting on Mathafurd's shoulder, pecked at him. 'Oh,' he said. 'Yes. We were going to send her a message, weren't we? Fly to Caer Criostal and find her then. Tell her we are on the way, and that the hounds are no longer a threat.' The hootcat flew off, keeping low to the ground. Mathafurd followed on foot. Neither owl nor dwarf noticed the small, menacing green cloud looming up on the horizon behind them. A double lightning flash, as of malevolent eyes watching, came from its depths.

Caer Criostal lay close above them as Linnet and Gilla and the Affank sneaked in silently under the castle, working their way upwards through a maze of dry underground storerooms containing barrels of grain, baskets of dried flower petals and assorted nuts, jars of berries and honey, trays of onions, carrots and odd-looking knobbly roots, among other more exotic things which Linnet did not recognise. It smelt wholesome and inviting after the foul caves below, although whiffs of Affank stink kept breaking through into Linnet's nostrils. The Affank swung between whimpering and licking its lips.

'Good food here,' it pleaded piteously behind them, over and over again. 'Affank is hungry.' But after a short conference with Gilla, Linnet made it walk in front, driving it on with a whispered threat. Her heart was still beating fast with fear, but her victory over the smelly beast had given her some necessary confidence in the efficacy of her Power, and she hugged her small triumph inside herself like a lucky talisman. On and on they went. There seemed to be no one around, although they had had one scary moment in the cellars when they had heard a lot of panicked shouting, cursing and running about above them. The Affank began to whine again, more loudly this time.

Linnet ran up behind the Affank and poked it till it turned round and looked at her, cringing. 'Shh!' she said and scowled at it fiercely till it shut up. Her mind drifted briefly to Vesterton Comprehensive. Perhaps it was a look that would work on Them. She somehow doubted it. They were a lot tougher than any Affank. Despite its ferocious appearance, it was all noise and bluster, she decided.

When the sounds had stopped, they continued. Up they climbed through the kitchens, where ladles and spoons lay idle in great cauldrons, all full to the brim. There was a buzzing, tingling feeling around the pots of food, which Linnet's instincts told her to stay well clear of.

'Stasis spell,' Gilla whispered. 'So the food won't go to waste. Looks like the whole bundle of them have run out to chase after you. Including the sorceress. A bit of luck at last. But I expect we'll pay for it in the end. Luck never comes for free.'

Linnet's eyes were out on stalks by the time they tiptoed up the rose-quartz staircase to Fidget Reedglitter's quarters at the top of the topmost tower. Caer Criostal was exquisite. They had flitted from floor to floor, hiding behind pillars and in doorways, just in case the Fey had left someone on guard. Their path lay always upwards, the Affank leading the way. Linnet had glimpsed a room full of lapis-coloured butterflies dancing a neverending dance around a giant spire made entirely of bluebells; she had crept past chambers and chambers decorated with moving patterns of glittering shell-jewels and spidersilk curtains so fine that they swayed at the least breath; she had seen the Fey Queen's throne – a calla lily carved out of one enormous pearl. Her mind buzzed with wonders until she could hardly think, only look and look and look, letting her feet take her automatically after her hairy guide. Gilla, however, was sniffing and muttering about such a waste of magic on decorations.

At the top of the rose-quartz staircase, the Affank stopped in front of a closed door.

'Here is room of Fidget Reedglitter,' it moaned. 'Bad place. Affank doesn't like it.' Scents of musty leaves, and old bones and something darker and fouler drifted out from underneath it, overpowering the flowery scents that dominated the rest of the castle.

Gilla sniffed. 'This is definitely Fidget's lair from the smell of it. Now, where's that necklace I heard Mathafurd telling you to make?' Linnet dug in her pouch and pulled it out. 'Go on then, girl. Put it on.'

'What's it for? Mathafurd wouldn't tell me,' Linnet asked, slipping the long string of red berries over her head. It smelt sharp, and lemony, and somehow safe.

'It will give you the protection of the Hulda for a short while – hide you from Feysight, should Fidget think to check what is happening here. The dwarf should have told you.' She passed her hand over the doorknob, which glowed a virulent green. 'Pah! A locking spell, carelessly done.' She took a feather from her cloak and brushed it over the lock, which immediately clicked and opened. 'Come on then, you've work to do.'

Linnet poked the Affank again, rather halfheartedly. It had become so pathetic and droopy by now that she was beginning to feel sorry for it. 'Stay there and warn me if anyone comes,' she hissed. Then she took a deep breath and followed Gilla over the threshhold, closing her eyes and expecting to be struck by Fidget's defences at any moment. But there was only silence. They had actually broken into the rooms of the Fey sorceress. Despite Gilla's permanent air of grumpiness, Linnet let out a muffled whoop of triumph. This was almost too easy.

'Result!' she whispered.

'That,' said Gilla repressively, 'remains to be seen.'

chapter thirteen

The Chalice of Athyr

Mar a bha As it was
Mar a tha As it is
Mar a bhitheas As it shall be
Gu brath Evermore

Runes written on the Chalice of Athyr

'Where do we start?' said Linnet, looking around at
the room. It was full of piles of strange-looking
leaves and roots and odd-coloured petals, as well as the
furs, dried skins and what appeared to be partially burnt
bones of various animals and birds. That accounted for
the smell. There was an ornate silver bed hung with dirty,
ripped thistledown curtains in one corner, which looked
wildly out of place, and several shelves and tables of
crystal bottles, pots and bowls, all filled with potions.
Some of them were bubbling wetly.

'*You* start,' said Gilla. '*I* am going to sit down and rest
my old feet. Hulda legs are not designed for hurry, nor for
all those stairs.'

Linnet had a moment of panic. Then she relaxed. She was the Maiden. She could do this. She was *meant* to do this. But how? Well? she demanded from the Maiden voices. How do we do this? There was a silence, and then an image of bees seeped out from the small door inside her head where the Maiden voices lived. Linnet shuddered. She didn't want to think about bees, and the terrible thing she'd done – when was it? Yesterday? It seemed like a lifetime ago. But they were right. She knew she could do a Summoning spell already. It was the obvious way to go. Yes, she'd Summon the Chalice. But she'd really have to concentrate, and it couldn't just be a straightforward spell. First she'd have to think of a clever way to find out where in the room Fidget had hidden it – if it was here at all. And she'd have to do it in such a way that Fidget wouldn't be alerted to her presence – she'd have to find a spell that Fidget didn't know about and wouldn't be expecting. And that meant technomagic.

'OK,' she said, thinking out loud. 'If it's in here, it will be protected. So first I need a witness – someone who saw what she did – what spells she used to hide it and protect it. Otherwise I'll just trigger something. But there's nothing here that can tell me – nothing alive anyway.' She went over to the pile of animal remains. 'Unless . . .' she looked down at her wrist, which had been empty of a watch since she entered Avvallon. Could she use her technomagic without the watch being actually present? There was only one way to find out. She turned to the seated Hulda.

'Does a powerful magic spell leave traces when it happens?'

'Yes,' said Gilla cautiously. 'It does. There is always an imprint for eyes to see that can. But how . . . ?'

'Good.' Linnet interrupted her, sounding more confident than she felt. 'Then I know exactly what I'm going to do.' She picked up a pathetically small piece of mouse fur and placed it carefully on the pile of tiny charred bones beside it. Then she closed her eyes and called up an image of her watch. It appeared immediately, insubstantial and misty, but there. She focused on it fiercely and laid her hand on top of the pile of skin and bones.

'Trobhad, an Luch!
Come, O Mouse!'

she said softly. Then she tapped into the image of her watch, blending in the technomagic with the Old magic spell bit by bit as she did so. This time it was much easier. Suddenly, beneath her hand was a wriggling and a joyous squeaking. 'Hello, Mouse,' she said, lifting it up onto her palm. 'Welcome back to your life.'

The mouse looked at her with a bright, beady eye. 'I was in bits,' it said suspiciously. 'The Fey caught me in here eating crumbs and . . .' it shuddered, remembering the horrors of dismemberment and fire.

'Well, you're back now, so just . . . try and forget about it,' she said gently. She paused, then looked at the mouse, willing this to work. 'If I am right about magic leaving traces around where it is cast, your fur will hold the memory of what happened in here during the time you were . . . er . . . not yourself,' said Linnet tactfully. 'And it will be much easier for me to See that now you are whole again. Will you let me use you to See with?'

'It can't be worse than what *she* did to me,' said the mouse resignedly.

'I promise it won't hurt,' said Linnet, smiling. She closed her eyes and concentrated hard on the mouse's fur. Small dots of colour fizzed at the end of each hair, coalescing, melding into each other until gradually an image formed. Fidget Reedglitter swam into focus.

The Chalice of Athyr was in the centre of a circle of leaves, and Fidget was staring at it intently. Then she raised her hand and pointed at it with a crystal twig, hung with feathers.

> '*Duir, Nion Ash and Quert Apple,*' she cried.
> '*Huath, Gort Ivy and Reed.*
> *Alter this metal to leaf, twig, and petal,*
> *Turn it to branch, root and seed.*'

The Chalice shimmered for a moment, then subsided into a pile of plant fragments. The Fey sorceress stooped and scooped it up with her bony hands. Then she whirled in a sudden movement, flinging the debris to all four corners of the room, where it fell with a soft patter. She cackled triumphantly. Then she raised the twig wand once more.

> '*If Chalice come whole, and I be not here,*
> *Bring water, Cirein Croin, and fishdemons of Fear!*'

Linnet broke the Seeing link with a shudder. Her Maiden voices gave her a picture of the Cirein Croin as the mouse leapt off her hand and scampered towards the door. 'I'm off to the woods,' it squeaked. 'Crumbs are good, but acorns are safer.'

'Good plan,' said Linnet absently. She was thinking hard. The Chalice was definitely here, but how on earth was she going to get round that last bit? And what were fishdemons? None of the Maiden voices had ever heard of them.

'Well?' Gilla's grumpy voice interrupted. 'What are you going to do. Even if you could put the Chalice back together, you'll have the Cirein Croin and a whole lot of fishdemons to deal with to boot. I'd just like to remind you that the Cirein Croin eats seven whales for breakfast every morning. She's got you, hasn't she – that Fidget?' Linnet whirled round. She had had quite enough. She was sick of being doubted by someone else – she did a very good job of doubting herself, thank you very much.

'If you can't be helpful, then just shut up,' she shouted. 'I'm thinking, in case you hadn't noticed.' Gilla subsided, muttering to herself once more. Then she looked up.

'It is my duty as the Gruff to show the side of darkness,' she said. 'I – I find it hard to do anything else.' Linnet nodded shortly. She knew that was all the apology she would get.

'Tell me about fishdemons, please, instead of grumbling so much,' she said. 'I don't seem to know about them.'

'Something the clever Maiden doesn't know about?' Gilla said sarcastically. 'Well, I suppose I'm of some use then.'

As she began to drone on about the small, fierce underwater beings who brought dread and panic wherever they were found, Linnet listened with one ear as she paced the small room, stepping carefully round the piles on the floor and thinking hard. She could put the Chalice together again, she reckoned. That would not be too difficult. Another Summoning spell, a simpler one this time, mixed with a Binding spell and a bit of technomagic should do it. But how was she going to deal with the aftermath?

'Does the Cirein Croin answer to anybody, or anything?' she asked Gilla abruptly, interrupting the flow of information on fishdemons. 'Is it possible to control it?'

'Control the largest sea serpent in the world? Who could do such a thing? Unless it is the King of the Merr himself. Yes, I suppose Ardath could control it, if he wanted to. But there's no use in it, so what's the point in asking?'

Linnet clenched her fists, willing her temper down once more. Gilla just couldn't help being pessimistic, she supposed, as her Maiden voices chattered at her again, showing her a childhood memory – her father reading from a big storybook. There was a picture she couldn't quite see, but it seemed to have a mermaid in it. Linnet frowned, trying to remember the story. It was important, she knew it was. Then it came. Just a fragment of recollection from long ago, but it was enough to trigger an idea.

'Does the Merr King like Fidget Reedglitter?'

'Well, no,' said Gilla grudgingly. 'He doesn't. Ever since his youngest daughter fell in love with the Fey Prince and begged her for legs instead of a tail so she could dance with him at the Midsummer Ball. Fidget gave them to her, but she took her voice as payment, and every time the poor girl took a step it was like knives cutting into her. It all ended badly, for the Prince knows better than to love anyone but the Fey Queen. Ardath has never forgiven Fidget for it and Ligeia Bright-Voice is still dumb as a piece of dead coral.'

Linnet nodded. That was it. The story of the Little Mermaid. It had been one of her favourites at bedtime. 'I thought I remembered something like that from my world,' she said, a plan evolving in her head as she spoke. 'I think the Merr King is the key to defeating the Cirein Croin, and if I've got this right he'll definitely help me – if I can get to him.'

'And how will you do that, pray? You may have some magic, I suppose, but the Merr King lives in the Caves of Lirrannan, at the bottom of the ocean, not here in Caer Criostal, in case you hadn't noticed. And what were you thinking of doing about the fishdemons that come with the Cirein Croin? I've just told you they bring fear and who knows what else. How will you deal with them?'

'Fear and fishdemons I can deal with, I think,' she said calmly, settling Cernunnos's cloak more firmly round her shoulders, and stroking the softness. A ripple of silver sparks flew out from it, and settled in her hair. 'And as for the other – I have a plan now. But it will only work if I do it alone.'

'And suppose I won't let you do it alone?' said Gilla.

But Linnet was determined. Her plan felt right, and she was going to carry it through. However much Gilla argued.

And Gilla did argue. When Linnet eventually told her exactly what she was going to do, Gilla's mouth dropped open and she fell silent for the first time since Linnet had met her. Linnet almost laughed at the ludicrous expression of shock that had appeared on Gilla's face.

'But . . . but . . . but . . .' the Huldawoman spluttered. Then she threw up her hands. 'You will destroy us all. But I see you will not be moved. Mortals are so stubborn. Don't blame me if it all goes horribly wrong – which it will, you know.'

'I won't,' said Linnet, shooing her out of the room gently. 'Now please go and find Mathafurd and Gladysant if you can, and tell them what's going on. Mathafurd'll worry otherwise. He did promise to send a message, but I think he must have forgotten – or the hootcat got lost on the way here. I do hope he's all right.'

'Huh!' Gilla snorted. 'That one would be all right if he was standing in the mouths of Hel itself. He can take care of himself. But I suppose I could do what you ask. It'll mean a terribly long detour – nights spent sleeping in poor, cold comfort most likely – but trouble for others means nothing to you, girl, does it?' She turned and patted Linnet swiftly on the shoulder, her grumpiness gone for a fleeting moment. 'Good luck, Maiden,' she muttered. 'You'll need it.' And then she was gone, stumping past the shivering Affank, and down the rose-quartz stairs.

Linnet heaved an exasperated sigh. 'What am I going to do with *you*?' she asked the hairy monster. 'You certainly can't stay here with me. It's far too dangerous, and you'd just get in my way.' The Affank whimpered and hid its face. It had felt the strength of Linnet's mouse spell, and it hadn't liked it at all. Its brain was not very big, but it was clever enough to know that powerful magic of that sort usually meant danger.

'Affank go back to cave?' it whined hopefully.

'Oh, very well,' said Linnet. 'But you have to promise not to tell anyone I was here, and not to leap on any mortals ever again. And you have to have a bath every week.' The Affank moaned in horror. It had a dim, distant memory of baths from when it was a cub. And it hadn't liked them then either. But perhaps the mortal wouldn't come and check on it . . . and if it went quickly, it could steal some food on the way.

'Affank promises,' it said, looking at her slyly.

'I'll know if you don't,' said Linnet sternly. 'Off you go, now.' The Affank bounded down the stairs at a rate of knots, leaving a trail of stink behind it. Linnet waved her hand under her nose.

'Eeuggh!' she said, and turned back into Fidget Reedglitter's rooms.

Sometime later, Linnet was standing inside a carefully constructed dome of air, hung with rowanberries. She was totally protected from anything outside it – at least that was what she hoped. She had Summoned the parts of plant that now made up the Chalice, and they lay in a pile at her feet.

'Now for the hard bit,' she said, breathing hard as she called on the image of her technowatch once more and cast the new spell she and the Maiden voices had worked so hard on creating.

Keeping it all together shook every bone in Linnet's

body. The feeling was so much more powerful than she had expected. The Binding spell bonded with the technomagic almost immediately, and then a golden light filled the dome as the Chalice reappeared, its atoms clicking into place one at a time until the cup stood whole at her feet. It was beautiful, but there was no time to admire it, nor to read the runes written on its side. Linnet reached out hastily, took it, and put it in her pouch. It was not a moment too soon. At once there was a rush of seawater and an angry roar, as Fidget's protection spell was triggered. The room filled with seawater. The head and tail of an enormous and unpleasantly surprised sea serpent appeared through the windows, thrashing violently and surrounded by a host of small fishdemons. Each demon carried a many-thonged whip which radiated fear and menace. They rushed forward and reached towards the dome, towards Linnet, snarling and snapping as they came. The lash of a whip broke through the air dome and curled round one of her ankles. The shock of fear was immediate – intense and horrifying despite the protection of Cernunnos's cloak, and then the Cirein Croin opened its vast jaws to engulf them all.

> *'An Mui! An Siaban!*
> *Cuir làmh an sinne!*
> *Oh Sea, Oh Seaspray,*
> *Seize us away!'*

cried Linnet urgently in the new spellwords she had prepared, battling panic. The room exploded outwards and at once Avvallon whirled around them as both she, the

Cirein Croin and the fishdemons disappeared, leaving behind only rubble and a ruinous gush of seawater to rush through Caer Criostal, soaking and destroying the carefully constructed bowers and decorations that had lain ready for the Fey Queen's return.

Fidget Reedglitter stood in front of the Door, her hands on her bony hips. The copper mist was as bright as ever, and she felt the strength of the spell pulsing in her bones. It felt *wrong*, she thought. And it was holding her Prince captive, and keeping her Queen from Avvallon. She raised her wand and let fly a great bolt of shattering magic. The mist shivered slightly, but otherwise remained unchanged.

'I will find whoever has made this abomination!' shrieked the sorceress. 'I will find them, and then I will kill them very slowly.' She licked her lips. 'And then I will serve them up at the Queen's Homecoming feast,' she whispered. 'In very, very small bits.' She threw another bolt of magic, but the Door just absorbed it. She could feel herself growing weaker. She was maintaining too many spells, and it was time to let some of them go. Then she stiffened. Someone was in her rooms. Someone had triggered the protection spell. 'Nooooo!' she wailed, as she felt the Chalice of Athyr come together, and then leave Caer Criostal almost in the same moment.

'My Prince,' she cried, running towards her airdragon. 'If you can hear me, I will return and free you – if I can. But for now, I go to punish the one who has caused this.' As the dragon leapt into the air, she tuned into her watch-cloud. Her eyes narrowed as she saw the figure of a running dwarf going in the direction of Caer Criostal.

'Follow and take him as he reaches the gate,' she snarled. 'I'm coming.'

The exhausted hootcat owl had been flying for what seemed like days when it reached Caer Criostal. It arrived just in time to see the topmost tower explode in an angry flood. It flapped upwards in shock, circling until the worst was over, and then flew down to a pillar and surveyed the damage. One wall of Caer Criostal had been blown out completely, and the courtyard lay under a swirling mass of dirty water, dotted with a flotsam and jetsam of wrecked garlands and flowers. It hooted sadly as it flew along deserted corridors, searching for Linnet. But it did not find her, so it settled down to wait for Mathafurd. When he arrived a good deal later, he stopped in shock. He knew this was Linnet's doing. Who else had the power to destroy Caer Criostal so comprehensively?

'What on earth has she done now?' he said out loud, smelling the taint of technomagic. 'And more importantly, where in Avvallon *is* she now?'

Suddenly he was engulfed from behind in a suffocating cloud of wet, green mist. Its amorphous grip held him tighter than any rope.

'Where is *who*, dwarf?' hissed a terrible voice from above. Fidget Reedglitter landed and stepped down from the back of her airdragon into the courtyard. 'Where is who? And how have they done these things in Avvallon? Oh! What pleasure I shall take in finding out from you before you die. And then I shall find and kill them too. The Queen shall have dwarf pie at her banquet – and other things. But not before I have all the truth!' Mathafurd felt the cloud release him for an instant, and then the agonising bite of magic chains as they wrapped around his body, and he fell helpless into a pool of salt-tasting water at Fidget Reedglitter's feet.

'Fly,' he shouted to the hootcat. 'Fly!' And then all was darkness and pain.

chapter fourteen

The Caves of Lirrannan

'*. . . that great sea-snake under the sea*
From his coiled sleeps in the central deeps
Would slowly trail himself sevenfold
Round the hall where I sate . . .'

Alfred, Lord Tennyson

It was not a good day for the Merr King, Ardath the Fifty-First, Lord of the Ocean Reaches, Stirrer of Storms, Calmer of Waves, Feeder of Fish, Protector of Pearls etc etc. Sometimes he felt he had too many titles, none of them any use to him at the present moment. Ligeia Bright-Voice, his youngest daughter, was going through one of her periodic attempts to speak, and as usual, nothing came out of her mouth but painful gruntings. At least she had her tail back – that much he had wrung out of the wretched Fey sorceress – curse her – but the voice was gone for ever, he feared, unless he could get his hands on the Chalice of Athyr and restore it. Lirrannan only knew what dreadful use Fidget Reedglitter had put the stolen voice to – but it was bound to be something foul. He patted Ligeia on the shoulder helplessly. The Chalice was out of his grasp as long as the sorceress had it and that was that.

Ardath stiffened and swivelled round, his hand tightening so that Ligeia squirmed away from him in discomfort. He opened his mouth to apologise. Then he heard panicked shouting and a muffled roaring coming closer and closer. His chamberlain swam frantically up to him.

'Come, Sire, please, quickly. The Cirein Croin is in the throne room with its demons. And another – a mortal girl.'

The throne room was so large that it usually dwarfed everyone and everything. But as Ardath swam in, it seemed suddenly small and cramped. This was not surprising, since the Cirein Croin was taking up most of the space in it.

'Hold!' he boomed, using his trident to send a calming spell to soothe the thrashing beast and still it before it knocked his whole palace to pieces. 'What is the meaning of this?' A mortal girl, wearing an embroidered doeskin cloak which reeked of magic, stepped forward within what looked to him like a domed bubble of air.

'Your Majesty,' she said, sinking to one knee. 'I'm very sorry for the intrusion. I am the Maiden, and I am escaping from Fidget Reedglitter. She stole this beast of yours for her own purposes, and I – I hoped you might be glad that I had brought it back to you.'

Ardath scowled. 'And what did the Fey sorceress want with a Cirein Croin. Does she not have enough power of her own without taking yet more from me?'

'She wanted it to protect this,' said Linnet, drawing out the Chalice of Athyr from her pouch.

'Oho!' said the king, laughing suddenly. 'If you have stolen that from her, you have given her a hurt such as she will not have suffered in an age! I like you already, mortal Maiden. You have brought me my only desire.' Then he turned to the Cirein Croin. 'Begone!' he said, 'and your fishdemons with you. Be at peace in the depths of ocean and trouble this mortal no more.' The huge sea serpent disappeared in a flash of silver, fishdemons clinging to its sides.

'Thank you,' said Linnet. 'Whew! That was a relief. I don't think it would have held off eating me for much longer.' The king was staring at her thoughtfully, almost hungrily. 'Er, your Majesty,' she said nervously, her voice echoing strangely in the bubble. 'You're not going to eat me yourself, are you?'

'No,' he said dreamily. 'No.' Then abruptly, 'Do you know what it is you carry? Yes, of course you do. But do you know what powers the Chalice of Athyr has?' Linnet looked at him properly for the first time. It was hard to tell, what with the green scaly skin and the seaweedy beard, but she thought he looked – well – like Mum looked sometimes when she was worried about something. Usually Dad overdoing it on one of the Brews, she thought with a pang of homesickness. She stuffed it down and answered the king.

'I know I need it to put the worldwyrm back to sleep. But I need the dragonwort elixir too.' She slumped forward despairingly. 'And now Fidget will be even more on the lookout than she was before, and I'll probably never be able to find it. But, no, I don't know if the Chalice does anything else.'

'I do,' said Ardath. 'There is an old Merrish prophecy, which I never understood till now. But it may just be time to test it.'

'Not another prophecy,' Linnet groaned. 'I'm sick of prophecies. Ones that are about me, anyway. And I suppose this one is?'

'Yes, I think so,' the king said. 'It goes like this . . .

> '*When Cup and Maid appear, afraid,*
> *then Voice shall sing, before the King.*'

'Summon Ligeia Bright-Voice,' he told the chamberlain. 'If I am right, it is time for her to sing again. Now, Maiden,' he said, coming towards her. 'You must help me use the Chalice to give my daughter back her voice.'

'And how on earth do I do that?' asked Linnet, just as a pretty Merr-girl swam into the throne room.

'I will show you,' said Ardath, reaching into the air bubble to take the Chalice from her. He traced a pointed green nail over the runes on its side.

> '*As it was,*
> *As it is,*
> *As it shall be,*
> *Evermore,*'

he murmured, reading the runes out loud. And Linnet felt the spell begin to resonate in her blood as she joined in, instinctively twining her voice around Ardath's as they chanted together, over and over and over again.

'*Mar a bha*
 Mar a tha
 Mar a bhitheas
 Gu brath,'

sang Linnet in high crystal tones she did not recognise as
her own.

The spell words rose from the Chalice into the green
water and formed into a whirling column of tiny, bright
silver bubbles which raced like an arrow towards the Merr
girl's throat and pierced it. She gave a great, hoarse cry.

'Father! Oh father! I have my voice back!' And as she
swam into Ardath's arms, she wept and laughed, all at the
same time.

The strains of the silver lap harp died away, and a clear,
achingly beautiful song rose to echo off the ceiling of the
banqueting hall. Once again Linnet sat at the king's right
hand, toying with her crab and seaweed soufflé (which she
didn't much like) and still wondering at being able to
breathe quite normally underwater. When her air dome
began to fail, quite soon after the first celebrations at the
return of Ligeia's voice, Ardath had sent for his personal
spell chest. He had opened it and poured her out a small
shellfull of something that tasted of fizzy seawater with a
bit of rosehip syrup mixed in. She had drunk it down, and
then the dome of air had been unneccesary. Ligeia had not
stopped singing since the Chalice had restored her. Well,
Linnet amended, actually she *had* stopped quite a few
times to hug and thank her rescuer. It had been a little
embarrassing, really, as well as quite slimy. Mermaid skin

was rather fish-like and scaly to cuddle up to. Linnet was still not absolutely sure what they had done, nor how – she and Ardath had sung the spell together in different ways for ages – but it seemed to have worked, and now Ardath had promised to help her find the elixir as a kind of thank you present. She felt rather relieved. She hadn't been looking forward to doing it on her own, and although she wasn't missing Gilla's grumps at all, she would have liked to have Mathafurd's sturdy and comforting presence at her side. Had Mathafurd got her message from Gilla? And if so, where could she find him? Perhaps the king would know. She thought back to her first proper conversation with Ardath, after he had handed her back the Chalice. She had had to explain about the worldwyrm and everything else all over again, but it had been worth it.

'If, as you say, Fidget has hidden the elixir in a pool,' he had said, 'it will be much easier. Any water being is ruled by me, and now that Ligeia's voice is restored, I will command them all to help you, and I will give you a waterspell to summon someone to retrieve the leech when you get there. But now, after you have rested for a little, we must have a celebration feast for seven nights and days. I absolutely insist, and anyhow, it's the traditional Merrish way of saying thank you. It's the least we can do.'

Linnet had been too overawed to say no to Ardath, who was quite regal and overpowering when he set his mind on something, and anyway it didn't seem polite to refuse. She knew that she should probably have protested that she needed to get on with her quest. But it was a novel feeling for Linnet to be fêted as a heroine, and she had succumbed quite easily to the deluge of admiration she had been showered with by Ligeia and her friends.

Merr people were huge fun to be with, Linnet decided, smiling to herself dreamily as she remembered how Ligeia and her two sisters and all their friends had insisted on showing her round the whole kingdom, with its amazing mother-of-pearl caves, and green seaweed forests where the sun shone golden-green through the clear blue water. She closed her eyes and saw once again fish like sparkling multi-coloured jewels, grazing in beds of swaying anemones.

'More samphire wine?' asked the king, bringing her back from her dream with a bump. Linnet shook her head politely.

'Er, no. No thank you, Your Majesty,' she said hurriedly. Samphire wine was truly vile, and Linnet had determined on the first night of feasting never to touch another drop. The king turned away from her, and Linnet fell back into her reverie. She couldn't decide what the best bit had been. Was it when she had ridden on a dolphin's back in the moonlight? Or having her hair done in the Merrish style and trying on the entire contents of Ligeia's sea-gem box, which was extensive, to say the least? Or was it the time when she got out her bottle of Airs and made herself and all the others invisible so they could sneak up behind all the best-looking Merr boys and pull their tails? She gave up, unable to choose.

It was just so nice to spend time with a load of other girls who actually seemed to like her and accept her for who she was. It made her feel special and normal, all at the same time. And they'd even complimented her on her hoodie (rather stained now, but thankfully the Maiden memories had come up with a spell to keep her clothes dry – even under water). All the Merr girls were now wearing hurriedly made copies, made out of bright pink sharkskin and decorated with pearls across the back. Linnet couldn't help grinning. The pearls read 'The Mayden Roks!' Well, they had asked her what the letters on her own said, and then adapted them in their own way. Merrish spelling seemed to be a bit eccentric – rather like hers. And that was another thing they had in common.

But time in the mortal world was ticking away, and she must find the elixir soon and face up to what she had to do there. It was now the seventh night of feasting, as far as she could work out from counting meals on her fingers, and she was getting more than a little restless, as well as feeling a bit guilty. Just how much time *had* passed since she entered Avvallon? Were her thirty days nearly up? She didn't think so, but it was still so hard to tell here. As she opened her mouth to ask the king when she could leave, and where he thought Mathafurd might be found, a flustered young Merrman swam up to the top table. Linnet knew him. He was rather handsome, and he had escorted her and the Merr princesses on one of their trips.

'Your Majesty,' he stammered. 'I was swimming by the rocks on the Eastern shore, when I heard an owl hooting. It was crying "Linnet, Linnet," which I know is the Maiden's name,' (here he blushed, which made Linnet blush too), 'so I called to it.' As the young Merrman blurted out the hootcat's news about Mathafurd's capture by the sorceress, Linnet felt a sinking feeling in her stomach. She had known all along she shouldn't have been tempted to stay here. And now Mathafurd was in trouble and she'd have to get him out. Him, Zafira, how on earth was she going to manage rescuing them, not to mention getting the Chalice, the elixir, herself and everyone home? It seemed an even more impossible task than it had before, and she felt a great lump of guilt land in her stomach with a crash that nearly made her vomit up what little she had eaten of her crab and seaweed soufflé. How could she have lingered here, enjoying herself, when her friends and family were in trouble?

chapter fifteen

Two Rescues –
and a Nasty Surprise

'. . . Thorough flood, thorough fire,
I do wander everywhere,
Swifter than the moone's sphere'

William Shakspear

The feast had dissolved into a flurry of action and orders and hurried farewells, and on the Merr King's command, Nixies and Seasprites and Wavegnomes had escorted her by watery routes all the way over leagues and leagues of sea. She had ridden on the back of swift-swimming dolphins and whales and all through the first day's travelling she had kept asking her escorts how far it was and when they would be there. She was desperately worried about Mathafurd, and wanted to rescue him as soon as possible. And also she was furious with Fidget Reedglitter and wanted to get even with her. Linnet didn't care any more how powerful and scary she was – the fear had somehow washed away with the realisation that she had already outwitted the sorceress once, and she could probably do it again. But as the journey went on and on and on, she felt a sense of urgency growing. Would she be too late to save the dwarf? And what would that mean for her quest? How much time did she really have left? She found it impossible to work out, however much finger counting she did. She squirmed with guilt yet again as she remembered how she had been enjoying herself with Ligeia, using Fay's Gift to have fun while Mathafurd languished in Fidget's clutches. *Why* hadn't she said no to Ardath and his endless feasts? Too much listening to Mum telling me to be polite to people, she thought. And then felt horribly homesick and worried about her parents. It was not a comfortable journey, with all the horrible thoughts roiling about in her head. And what made it worse was that the Maiden voices had gone silent. She very much feared that they were blaming her for what might be happening to Mathafurd.

'How far now?' she asked yet again, as they left the sea, and swerved into a river estuary.

'The bounds of Avvallon are wide and endless,' said a blue Wavegnome. 'But it is less than a day's ride from here.' Her dolphin steed slowed and headed for the bank.

'Why are we stopping?' she asked. But the answer was apparent immediately. A huge silvery salmon hovered in the water beside her.

'This is where I leave you,' said the Wavegnome. 'Finnegas will take you up to Caer Criostal from here.' Linnet flipped her legs over the dolphin's side and flopped rather ungracefully onto the salmon's back.

'Hang on,' he bubbled, and she felt the powerful muscles flex under her thighs as they darted upriver. As the banks flashed by in a blur, Linnet realised just how very far her spell had taken her. She hadn't thought before now about how huge Avvallon really was, and despite her regrets at having stayed with the Merrpeople for so long, she thanked Ardath in her mind. She could never have done this journey without his help. She would never have found the way.

The salmon swam on and on up miles and miles of river and stream until Caer Criostal was in sight. Then it had delivered her to a large clump of reeds where she found herself handed over to a Naiad called Iris. Linnet felt damp and irritable and as if she never wanted to see a drop of water ever again. Even her keeping dry spell wasn't totally infallible in the face of so much sea and river. She was also very tired – sleeping on the way had been almost impossible, although she had dozed a little on the broad back of a whale.

Caer Criostal stood nearly as empty and ruined as she had left it, but now a palpable air of menace hung over it. Fidget Reedglitter was now in residence, and she was obviously not happy. The clear aquamarine walls of the castle were clouded, and obsidian streaks radiated out from the topmost tower.

'That's where she'll have your friend,' whispered the Naiad, pointing and shuddering. 'Up there in her torture chamber.'

'Then that's where I'll rescue him from,' said Linnet.

'But . . . but . . . that's Fidget Reedglitter in there!' Iris said in a trembling voice. '*Fidget Reedglitter!*' She shuddered again, drops of water flying from her blue hair and settling in a ring of ripples around her. 'You *can't* – she'll kill you or something worse.'

Linnet was utterly fed up with being told what she could and couldn't do by now. Who did these idiots think she was?

'Just watch me,' she said, grim determination in her voice. It was time to show these people what the Maiden could do when she put her mind to it. A chorus of voices cheered inside her head, and she sighed in relief. They were back. 'Thanks, girls,' she whispered inwardly. 'Let's do this right now.'

A small breeze was playing in the rushes, and she Summoned it with a flick of her finger. 'Take me there,' she commanded it. And then she used the Smith's spell to turn herself into a spark, and floated upwards towards the topmost tower. She landed on the windowsill and looked around, her eyes fiery microscopic pinpricks. There was Mathafurd, hung high from the roof in a tarnished silver cage, chained and helpless, his clothes torn and burned, and with a nasty-looking black eye and blood on his cheeks, arms and legs. There was Fidget Reedglitter, stooped intently over a brazier, heating a stained and cracked pot which emitted sluggish grey smoke that floated downwards and hung in greasy swirls over the floor at her feet.

Linnet floated upwards again, and landed on Mathafurd's shoulder. 'It's me, Linnet,' she murmured against his ear. 'I've come to rescue you.'

Mathafurd opened his eyes and blinked painfully. 'Good,' he whispered.

Immediately, the Fey sorceress whipped round. 'What

was that, dwarf?' she snarled. 'Ready to talk are you?'

'No!' he said defiantly. 'Never! You old Fey toad!'

'Well you will be when this little gift is ready,' she said, stirring the pot menacingly.

Linnet felt white hot rage flare in her spark heart. Fidget Reedglitter was just a particularly nasty bully she realised – the Avvallon equivalent of Lelicia Sundew magnified a million times. And she had to be dealt with right here and now or the Maiden would fail. She knew she couldn't allow that to happen.

The spark Linnet settled on Mathafurd's chains, melting each with an intense burst of heat. They slithered through the bars of the cage with a loud jangling, and fell down onto Fidget Reedglitter's head as she stared upwards in shocked surprise, stunning and putting her out of action momentarily with their residual magic. Her mouth opened to cast a blasting spell as Linnet sped to the floor, and resumed her normal shape, pulling out her bottle of Airs as she did so.

> *'Trobhad, an stob reòtha!*
> *Come, Icicle!*
> *Reoth, O ban-bhuidseach!*
> *Freeze, O sorceress!'*

she cried, shaping a strand of white skyforce into ice-daggers before Fidget could utter a sound. The sharp shards of ice rushed from her fingertips, impaling the sorceress until she looked like a white hedgehog. Then a sheet of freezing water erupted from nowhere, encasing her in a block of blue-tinged ice, and immobilising her totally.

Linnet summoned the image of her technowatch to float on top of the ice block. Then she laid her hand on it, her palm burning with cold at the contact.

'Be Ice till Time end,'

she chanted, weaving old and new magic in unbreakable bonds.

> *'Break not, nor bend.*
> *Melt not, nor flow, let it be so.*
> *Be Ice till Time break — let this be your Fate.'*

She felt the spell take and hold as she uttered the last word. A shimmering rainbow veil now surrounded Fidget Reedglitter's prison, turning her evil to beauty. And as her malign influence was shut away from the room and died, the obsidian streaks faded from the walls, and the aquamarine tower shone bright again in the sudden sunlight.

'Well,' said Mathafurd Llewellyn from above. 'I don't think *she'll* be going anywhere for a while. That was quite a performance. Now, perhaps you could get me and Gladysant out of here. And find my harp.'

Linnet laughed, knowing deep inside herself that she'd never allow herself to be afraid of a bully again. She walked over to the pulley on the wall, and let the cage down slowly to the ground. The lock snicked open as she whispered to it, and Mathafurd stumbled out.

'I'm sorry,' she whispered, hugging him gently. 'Are you OK?'

'My own carelessness,' he said, shrugging and wincing

at the same time, as the movement caught the burns across his shoulders. 'I didn't see her coming. That ruddy cloud of hers must have been following me all along, and it sneaked up on me. Now, Maiden. What next? Gladysant and I are at your service.'

'Now,' said Linnet, 'we find the elixir, rescue Zafira and go home.'

'Not so fast,' said a grumpy voice from the doorway. 'Never a thought between the pair of you as to where that blessed elixir is hidden. How are you going to find it, eh? I didn't come up all those stairs again just to be left behind.'

'Gilla!' cried Linnet.

'Cousin!' shouted Mathafurd.

Gilla snorted. 'Get that lazy Beast of yours off your arm, and let's go. Time is running out, and that puny Door spell you did won't last for ever, I don't suppose. *I* haven't spent my time gadding about with princesses, having my hair done and trying on sea-gems like some people I know. Nor did I let a miserable little fluffy cloud capture me. I've been waiting and watching and gathering information instead. Lucky for you you've got someone sensible around, or this whole thing could have gone even worse. It's bad enough as it is, and not likely to improve.'

Linnet grinned at the familiar tones of doom and gloom. Perhaps she had missed Gilla a bit after all. Mathafurd winked at her as he poked Gladysant. She thought he might be quite happy to see Gilla too.

Avvallon stretched out under Gladysant's wings. It looked drier and deader and definitely a lot greyer than when

Linnet had first arrived. And it seemed to be getting a lot colder. Linnet frowned. It was distinctly odd. 'What's happened to the land?' she asked Gilla. 'It's gone all weird.'

The Huldawoman sighed. Her voice was sad – resigned almost – and she spoke more gently than usual. 'The Queen's return has been delayed, and the earth feels it. She is tied to this land, and as she ages, so does it. It is no longer eternal summer here. And now Fidget Reedglitter is powerful no more, her holding spells are all unravelling. I told you – we all pay a heavy price for your use of new magic and old here in Avvallon. But the wyrm must be contained or we will all die in every world. This is why we help you. Now,' she said in her normal voice, 'turn left at that patch of red poppyflowers. We are nearly there.'

After Gilla had directed Gladysant down to land at the pool by Fidget's hut, Linnet had used the waterspell summons Ardath had given her as she left the Caves of Lirannan. Very swiftly he had sent two burly Rivergnomes to dive into the murky green depths of the mud pool where Fidget had dropped the bespelled leech with the elixir inside. They had fished around for long minutes, but at last they had resurfaced, carrying the long, slimy black bag, which they had handed to her hurriedly, and run off to find some clean water to bathe in. The giant leech was just as unpleasant to touch as Linnet had feared it would be. At least she hadn't had to actually retrieve it, she thought, as she manhandled it into her pouch, where it plopped to the bottom, oozing unpleasantly.

'Eeugh! Eeugh! Eeugh!' she said, kneeling and wiping her fingers on a tussock of grass. 'I'm so glad I turned that foul Fey toadwoman into a permanent block of ice. This is just too gross and icky.'

Wayland's Gift really was amazing, she thought as she closed it over the disgusting mess inside. From the weight of it, there might as well be nothing in there at all, despite the fact that she was carrying a golden chalice and a very fat leechthing, as well as the rest of her Gifts.

As Linnet got up and walked over to where Mathafurd and Gladysant were waiting, Woodcock flew down to Gilla's shoulder and poked his long beak at her ear. After a lot of tssking and tutting from the Huldawoman, he flew off again, and Gilla came towards them.

'You must hurry,' said Gilla. 'The music girl is still on the Queen's Mound, and she is safe for now. But something strange is happening at the Door. I told you that spell of yours wouldn't last. And the rowanberries are dropping in my woods. Winter is coming. I must return to my people before it is too late – if it isn't already.'

'Thank you, Gilla,' Linnet said, giving her a hug. 'I'm sorry I've been such a pain in the neck. Really. And I hope your woods recover.'

'Hmmph!' said Gilla. 'Get on with you then.' But Linnet could tell she was pleased.

After Mathafurd had said his own farewell, they climbed up onto the waiting Gladysant's back, and soon they were soaring upwards. The land below seemed even greyer than before, if possible, and a depressing mist was creeping over the ground, covering every landmark. It was freezing cold and Linnet shivered and hugged Cernunnos's cloak close about her shoulders.

'Fly quicker, Gladysant,' cried Mathafurd. And

Gladysant's pink wings beat like a rushing gale as they hurtled on towards the Fey Mound, where Zafira was held captive. As they approached it, a thin thread of music rose into the air. Linnet recognised it at once as the piece she had heard coming out of the Feyglass, what felt like weeks ago. Actually, she realised, it probably was weeks ago. More than ever now, she wasn't entirely sure how long she had been in Avvallon for, but it definitely seemed like a very long time. Suddenly her magical instincts were screaming and a worrying sense of urgency possessed her again, even more intensely than before. What had been happening at home? Had the wyrm risen truly? And how were the Guardians coping with it? Were her parents and Petroc all right? And what was the Fey Queen doing? She squeezed her eyes tight shut, suddenly feeling a terrible rush of homesickness for all that was loved and familiar. But there was work to do, and so she squashed it back inside as best she could. Worrying wasn't going to get the wyrm back into its bed – nor save the worlds. The Maiden voices whispered to her comfortingly, but, she thought rather bleakly, she didn't think there was going to be much comfort where she had to go now.

'Come on,' she said to Mathafurd. 'I have a bad feeling that they need us on the other side of the Door. Let's get her and get out of here.'

They landed on the Mound and walked up to Zafira quietly. The girl seemed quite unaware of where she was and what she was doing. Her face was blank and calm and unknowing, and she didn't acknowledge Linnet's presence even when Linnet spoke to her.

'We'll have to do this together,' said Mathafurd. 'One,

two, three . . .' Linnet tugged Zafira's bleeding fingers off the 'cello strings and, with Mathafurd's help, pushed and pulled her unresisting body onto Gladysant's back. Hound voices whined complainingly about heavy loads and fat dwarves and Maidens, but the pink wings flapped laboriously into the air, and headed for the Door.

The creeping mist made it hard to see where they were going, and even worse, it had now started to snow. Fat, freezing flakes fell through the air, whipping into their cold faces, and the hound voices began to howl miserably. Linnet ignored them, reaching out with her magical senses, and soon she could feel her spell. There was something odd about it, but she couldn't work out exactly what it was. Maybe it was failing, as Gilla had predicted. Her heart began to beat fast again. What if the Fey Queen had broken through? She didn't want another fight on her hands. She felt so tired. Then she sat up straighter. There was the copper mist that marked the spot where the Door lay, and soon Gladysant had glided down to the ground in front of it. The snow lay there, thick and heavy and unmarked. But as they landed, a snarling pack of dogs erupted from the low-lying bushes around, scattering white powder as they came, and a host of green figures rose up out of the ground to surround them. All unnoticed in the furore, a hootcat landed on Gladysant's ear.

'Going somewhere?' mocked a drawling voice. 'I think not!' And the Fey Prince stepped out of the mist, crunching over the snow to stand in front of them. His face was tight with rage, and green blood ran down his body through the many tears and rents in his clothes. 'Did you think your new magic could hold me forever? I freed myself from it in the end, you see, though it cost me nearly everything I had and fighting it weakened Fidget Reedglitter almost to fading. I suppose the fact that you are here means that she is . . . incapacitated?' Mathafurd made a movement forward on Gladysant's back, but Linnet put her hand on his arm. This was a mess she had made, and she would deal with it in her own way – she had earned the right to make her own decisions by now.

She thought quickly. There was no time to consult her Maiden memories or to get anything out of her pouch. She would just have to rely on the Badger's Gift and her own Power. If ever she'd needed strength of both body and spirit it was now, and so she closed her eyes and called up the golden mist inside herself, feeling it roil and boil in her blood as she climbed down from Gladysant to stand in front of the angry Fey. The snow came up to her ankles, and she could feel the cold of it seeping into her trainers. His eyes looked at her, so old and so wise, but with her senses all on alert, she also caught a hint of weariness and defeat in them, for all his heated words. Perhaps . . . just perhaps . . . she had a chance.

'I am sorry for your hurts,' she said, using the Gift to make her voice sound strong and sure and full of Power. 'But I did what I had to as Maiden, and I don't make any apology for that. I couldn't risk the Queen coming through and joining forces with you to stop me. You know perfectly well the old magic isn't enough to contain the wyrm any more – you've used it and used it and now it just doesn't work properly in the modern world. That may be partly the fault of humans and our technostuff. But you

Fey . . . you know – you've always known – what is needed to put the wyrm back to sleep if it wakes, and yet you think of nothing and nobody but yourselves! All you've ever used the Chalice and the elixir for is keeping the Queen young and beautiful because that's all that seems to matter to you. Every Maiden there's ever been has had to fight Fidget Reedglitter to get them away from your so-called "guardianship" – I know – I have all their memories. And . . . and . . . it's not *right*!' she yelled passionately, in a righteous rage herself now. It felt good to have someone to yell at properly – someone who she thought – hoped – might actually understand.

'If the worldwyrm destroys the mortal world, how long do you think Avvallon will last? It's already dying because the Queen isn't here, and I don't feel very good about all the winter stuff. But you've no one but yourselves to blame. There has to be a balance between all the worlds and none cannot exist without the others. At least my kind of new magic gives us the first chance we've ever had of putting the wyrm out of time so it can sleep for ever. Don't you want that? Don't you want your punishment to end?' She stopped. Waited.

'Pretty words,' snarled the Prince. 'But how do I know they are true?'

'They are true,' said a deep voice behind him. A voice that echoed with the sound of falling rocks and water roaring. Cernunnos stepped forward seemingly from nowhere, his hooves sinking silently into the snow, to stand beside Linnet. He pointed a finger at the Prince.

'Can you not feel it? The old is passing away, and the

new joins with it and emerges stronger. This Maiden is without doubt the first of a different breed of mortal – I do not know how, but it is so. I too doubted her at first. But I have spoken to the Hulda now and I see that she has only done what she had to here, and that her Power is something good. I also know that she is our last chance. Come through the Door with her and lend us your aid for the last time. Then return to Avvallon and I will give you and your Queen a hunt of the Royal White Hart such as has never been seen since the time of legend.'

There was a murmuring of surprise and delight from the Fey Host surrounding them. But the Prince still looked suspicious.

'How do I know you will keep your word, Stagman?' he said contemptuously. 'You are bound to *her*, are you not? You are a Guardian, sworn to protect her. How do I know you are not lying, just to get her through the Door and away.' The air grew dark and menacing, and smelled of lightning.

'Because,' said Cernunnos, and now his voice rang with the bellow of a thousand rutting stags, 'I *am* the White Hart. When the wyrm sleeps once more, I will meet you in this place, and you must catch me if you can.' And before their eyes, he changed into a huge white stag, which towered over the Prince, menacing him with its many-tined horns. The Fey Hounds bayed triumphantly and crept forward, but the Prince motioned them back. He sighed, suddenly remembering his thoughts before the Door had caught him in its spell. Maybe, just maybe, this was the chance he had been wishing for. If not . . . he didn't want to think about if not.

'Very well,' he said. 'The Fey will enter the mortal world for the last time. And then it will be over. The Queen will return to us, and everything will be as it was before mortal mischief set us on this path.' He stepped back from the Door, and beckoned Linnet forward.

'Work your new magic then, Maiden,' he said. 'Open the Door. The Fey are yours to command.' Then he bent his head, and looked directly into her eyes, holding them with his own as if they were bound together with an invisible thread. 'But know this, Maiden,' he hissed. 'If the Queen dies, and Avvallon with her, then I will hunt you down instead of the White Hart. And you and your new magic will die as if they had never come into being, whatever the consequences.'

Linnet bowed her head. 'Let it be so,' she said. But her heart was beating so fast she could hardly think. The snow was falling more heavily than ever, and she very much feared that the Fey Queen might now be beyond hope of saving. 'Come on,' she thought to the voices inside her head. 'Show me the spell. Show me what you all did to put the worldwyrm back to sleep.' And as she raised her right hand to open the Door, they did.

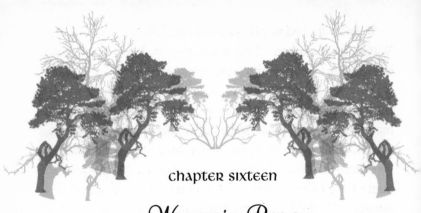

chapter sixteen

Wyrm's Rise

'The wyrm is shaken with giant rage,
for its hour hath come. It writhes
and wallows at Earth's heart, and it
rears its head in destruction.'

From 'The Prophecies of the Seven'

*S*econds after he had found the torn-apart car, Wayland saw the footprints. Two pairs of them, leading in the direction of the River Ash. And beside them a badger's distinctive track. He revved the motorbike.

'They're this way,' he shouted to Petroc over his shoulder. 'Let's go.' The motorbike skidded and slid across the thick mud of Black Meadows, following the trail all the way down the banks of the river to Inigo's Weir. Two figures were huddled there, staring into its depths. There was no sign of the Badger. They looked up at the sound of the machine.

'Merrilin, Nyneve! Over here! Come quickly!' Linnet's parents ran over to the bike.

Merrilin looked at his oldest friend. 'What is going on, Wayland?' he asked. 'Linnet has disappeared, and if you have young Petroc with you, you'll know about Zafira. Nyneve swears there's been some large animal following us, and Black Meadows has a creepy feeling about it – not to mention that the Bickerspike farm seems to be a pile of rubble. I know this is Wyrmesbury, but still . . .' he paused. 'We came down here because . . . because we thought Linnet might have fallen in and . . .' He didn't voice the rest of the sentence. He didn't need to. Too many drowned bodies had been found up against Inigo's Weir over the years.

'Linnet and Zafira are safe – or at least out of our reach,' said the Smith. 'But you two and Petroc are not safe. I have to get you out of here before . . . ' he hesitated.

'Before what, Wayland?' demanded Nyneve, her voice high and panicky. 'Tell me before what, right now.'

He sighed. 'We really don't have time for explanations. But briefly, I am a Guardian – yes, one of those from the old stories, Merrilin – and if you lot don't leg it into another dimension as fast as possible, you'll get eaten by a gigantic dragon wyrm thing that's buried just over there. Did you think Wyrmes*bury* got its name for nothing? Didn't you ever wonder what our earthquakes were caused by? Now come here, and keep quiet. I have to concentrate.' Behind him the ground started to shift and slip. The air began to tremble and grow hot. Nyneve opened her mouth to scream as one red-slitted wyrm eye emerged from the earth.

'*Fosgail Eadar,*' roared the Smith, shaping a door in the air. He pushed the three mortals through, and then, '*Duin!*' he cried desperately, wrenching it shut as a blast of fire swept towards them. Utter peace descended suddenly, and the chaos was contained on the other side.

'Where on earth is this?' asked Petroc faintly. He looked around. They were in a round green glade, surrounded by oaks. There was a pool in the middle, with an island on which one huge ash tree grew, its branches towering into the sky, its top so high that it pierced the clouds. Cradled unnoticed among its roots lay the small, still figure of Magret Bickerspike, dressed all in shimmering white. She looked as if she were sleeping.

'Nowhere on earth,' said the Smith, tiredly. 'This is the Gateway between the Worlds, and that is Iggdrasyl, the tree whose roots bind the Worlds together. It is the centre – all places and none. You will be safe here.'

'And how does my friend, the car mechanic, know about getting to such a place?' asked Merrilin quietly. 'Who are you, Wayland? I thought I knew you. We grew up together, dammit!' His voice grew louder. 'What has happened to my daughter?'

'Believe me, I want to tell you,' said Wayland. 'But there is no more time. You'll just have to trust me. Please, Merrilin. If I don't go back to Wyrmesbury now and help the other Guardians, the wyrm will destroy everything. It may still, but we have to try, so that Linnet will have a chance when she gets back. Petroc will tell you all he knows, which I suspect is a great deal.'

Merrilin picked up on the one thing he had heard properly. The rest was just too confusing to take in. 'What has Linnet got to do with this? When she gets back from *where*? *WHERE IS SHE?*' Wayland was already shaping another door.

'Linnet is the Maiden Guardian,' he said despairingly. 'No one but her can put the worldwyrm back to sleep. She's in Avvallon. I'm so very sorry.' Then the spell took hold and he disappeared back into the mortal world again. The air door vanished with a soft *shush*, and the three mortals were left alone on the other side.

'I think you'd better fill us in on what you know, Petroc dear,' said Nyneve, her voice deceptively soft. 'And after that I'm going to think up ways to kill Wayland Smith for getting my daughter involved in this.'

'Only after I've finished with him,' said Merrilin grimly.

Petroc sighed. 'I don't think it's as simple as that,' he said. And he began to tell them all he knew.

'Fires be thanked,' said Wayland, as he stumbled out onto Hootcat Hill and saw Professor Hullart. 'Where are the others?'

'Cernunnos has gone through to Avvallon by a different way to watch over Linnet,' he said. 'So we will have to do without him. The Badger is on his way from Black Meadows, as are Fay and the Lady. The Fey – well the Fey are there.' He pointed to the largest Owlstone. The ground at its feet was knee deep in filmy green bodies, all apparently unconscious. 'They streamed up just after Linnet . . . did what she did. This is my place of Guardianship, so I challenged them. I knew the Queen's power would be weak from so long in the mortal world – the Prince would have been a different matter. I told her that the Changeover would have to wait, that it was her duty to try and stop the wyrm till Linnet came back. We had quite an argument. But I could see her growing older

– she was fading before my eyes. Linnet's time spell must have done something to her anti-ageing magic. She and her Host became frantic, and threw themselves against the Door, trying to get through. Then Linnet's magic seized them and threw them back as you see them now. I don't think they are going to be very much help to us.' As he finished speaking, there was a sound of hooves, and Rhiannon burst through into the circle, the Badger and Fay behind her.

'It rises!' she cried. 'Beware! The wyrm rises.' They looked over towards Black Meadows where a huge shadow swayed high above the hills and threatened to blot out the sun. Fire streamed from its jaws.

The five remaining Guardians looked at each other in horror. Then they formed a linked spellcircle of quiet desperation. It was all there was to do now. '*DÌON!*' they cried as one. The shield magic rose over Wyrmesbury and set hard. The worldwyrm crashed into it and reeled back, causing the earth to judder and shake. It roared so loudly that the grass flattened from the very sound of it. 'Hold it steady,' said the Professor through gritted teeth. 'It will come again soon.' On and on the nightmare went as the minutes ticked past, but the Guardians held firm.

'How long,' gasped Fay. 'How long did Linnet say she'd be?' The Professor shook his head.

'Half an hour at most, and it's nearly been that already. I – I can't . . .' His eyes glazed over suddenly and he fell with a cry. The shield retreated and grew smaller, and the raging wyrm moved closer to Wyrmesbury. They could hear terrified screams rising from the town on the faint breeze blowing towards them. They could also smell the wyrm's stink – brimstone and sulphur and old, rotten things from the heart of the world, long forgotten deaths come to light on a bright May morning.

And then the Door to Avvallon opened with a screeching of metal and a scream of copper smoke. Linnet burst through, trampling the ethereal Fey bodies underfoot without even noticing, as her technowatch flew from the centre of the Door and fixed itself around her wrist. She had the Chalice of Athyr in one hand and the leech pouch of elixir in the other, and she was followed by the Fey Prince and his Host, Cernunnos, and Mathafurd Llewellyn on the Beast Gladysant, with a vacant-eyed mortal clinging to his back, and a hootcat fluttering behind.

'I am here, O Wyrm of the World,' she cried in its own language, her girl voice now a Summoning filled with the deep Power of earthflame and volcano. And the world-wyrm heard her.

chapter seventeen

Wyrm's Fall

Firesong in daylight.
Silver in wyrm's night
Sleep like death
Dream Maiden's breath.

From 'The Prophecies of the Seven'

$\mathcal{T}$he wyrm was silent for a long, waiting moment. Then it surged towards Hootcat Hill, over the River Ash, its unimaginably huge body ripping itself from the earth's heart, smashing hedge and field and everything in its way as it sought out the One who had called it.

'Are you mad?' rasped the Smith. 'What are you *doing*?'

Linnet looked at him calmly. 'What I was born to do,' she said. And she turned to look behind her. 'Distract it,' she ordered the Fey Prince, who was kneeling by his Queen's body. And then, turning to Mathafurd, 'Will you lend me Gladysant?'

He looked at her, troubled. 'Do you know what you are doing?' he asked.

She smiled ruefully. 'When have I ever known what I was doing? But yes, this time I think I do.' Mathafurd gave her a leg up.

'Be careful,' he said squeezing her ankle. But he knew that Linnet could not be careful. Not where she was going.

The Fey Host and their Prince rose into the air, their bodies now changed to ethereal wisps of green as they climbed towards the wyrm's head. They began to whirl and spin, dancing faster and faster until they were a green blur, travelling against the breeze at a speed faster than possibility. Linnet, too, rose on Gladysant's back. There were no complaining hound voices here, but she could feel a fierce eagle joy vibrating through the Beast's feathers. 'I'm so glad you want to be a hero!' she whispered. 'I'm not sure I do. But I don't have a choice right now.' She clung on with her knees as she fumbled with the golden Chalice and the leech full of elixir.

'*Fosgail! Open!*' she commanded, and the leech's mouth burst open, spilling most of the elixir into the Chalice. It began to fizz and bubble at once, and Linnet found it hard to keep it from spilling as the buffeting wind surrounding the worldwyrm caught Gladysant's wings. She dropped the leech back into her pouch, and grasping the full Chalice in one hand, took her technowatch off her wrist with her teeth, attaching it to one handle, threading the strap through and buckling it securely. The Chalice changed shape at once, becoming silver, angular and modern. New technorunes flickered on its side. Linnet read them silently.

The Fey Host were expiring now in large numbers, burning in oily green gouts of flame as the worldwyrm roared its fury at their distracting magic. Linnet was very near now. Her eyes were not wide enough to take in the enormity of the thing she had to conquer. There was no sun now, only darkness and chaos and the vile, whirling wyrmwind that spewed forth from the colossal mouth under the slitted golden-red eyes. Her heart was thunder, and she could feel the voices of every Maiden there had ever been urging her on inside her mind. She closed her eyes. Now. She had to do it now.

'Thanks, Gladysant,' she said. 'Wait for me!' And then she threw herself off the Beast's back towards the worldwyrm, screaming the newly-made spell she hoped against hope would work.

'*O bright dream Maiden, become a blazing light,*' she yelled in both the new language and the old. And turned into a flame Maiden, hurtling upwards towards the open jaws of the worldwyrm. She felt the soothing, drowsy music of the Fey pluck at her for a moment, then she was through and in. Intense heat seared her own blazing heart with inconceivable pain, and her fire hair crackled ominously on her head as she stood balanced on the tip of the vast tongue for the one small moment she had left before it swallowed her. She raised the Chalice high, breathed on its contents and poured the elixir down the worldwyrm's throat, remembering the new and old rune-words which she had read on its sides a long moment before. She opened her flame mouth to speak . . .

> '*Mar a bha*
> *As it was*
> *You are a fire*
> *And a devastating hunger*
> *Mar a tha*
> *As it is*
> *You will be a guarding sleep eternal*
> *Till Time spins out no more*
> *Mar a bhitheas*
> *As it shall be*
> *From every past*
> *To every future*
> *Gu brath*
> *Evermore!*'

she gabbled, chanting out old runes interwoven with her own technomagic to make a new spell of hope for the Time yet to come. Then she fled, fire out of fire, feeling the shock of shutting jaws at her blazing heels. On she plunged towards Gladysant's back, muttering the counterspell to turn her back from flame to mortal just before she landed. There was a smell of scorched feather and fur as Linnet looked up, no longer fire, but herself again. Then came the stillness and silence that occurs at the end of a great magic.

The worldwyrm's eyes closed, and it let out a sigh. Its huge body slithered downwards, swirling as water does when it goes down a plughole. Faster and faster it descended into the shaking earth, dragging pieces of ruin down with it – a hedge here, a stand of trees there – fences, walls, hills, valleys. In the blink of an eye it had disappeared deep beyond imagining, curling itself back around its true place as guardian of the earth's heart. Death and devastation lay behind it, but it was truly gone, and the earth was finally safe as it had not been since the wyrm first rose into the world above.

chapter eighteen

Endings

How calm, how beautiful comes on
The stilly hour, when storms are gone!
When warring winds have died away,
And clouds, beneath the glancing ray,
Melt off, and leave the land and sea
Sleeping in bright tranquillity.

Thomas Moore from 'Lalla Rookh'

As she clung on to Gladysant's back, Linnet was suddenly desperately tired, and she wanted to go home more than anything else in the world. But as soon as she and Gladysant landed back in the middle of the Owlstones, the Fey Prince materialised from the air beside her, his body now burned as well as bloody, and his face streaming with tears that looked like mist. She clutched the Beast's pink wings so hard that Gladysant turned and looked at her in reproach. It wasn't enough, she thought rather hysterically, that she had just put the worldwyrm back to sleep forever. Now she obviously had to deal with all the stuff that happened afterwards as well. It just wasn't fair.

'My Queen!' the Prince screamed at her. 'My Queen! Bring the Chalice, Maiden, or she will die!'

Linnet tumbled off Gladysant's back, ignoring the shouts of the other Guardians, and ran as fast as she could after the Prince, fumbling her watch off the Chalice handle and back onto her wrist as she stumbled and slipped on insubstantial green bodies. The Chalice didn't turn back into its old form when she did so, though. It simply remained silver and modern-looking. The Prince crouched down by the Door, and for the first time Linnet saw the Fey Queen in reality. Her body was no longer green. Nor was it really there anymore. Frost now covered it, and the icy crystals shaped like flowers were the only thing that made her outline visible on the trampled grass. The Fey Prince looked at her with pleading eyes.

'The elixir,' he whispered. 'Tell me there is some elixir left . . . please!' Linnet groped quickly in her pouch, hardly noticing the sliminess of the now-flabby leech body as she ripped it out and tipped it, mouth downwards, into the Chalice.

One . . . two . . . three . . . four . . . five . . . six . . . seven painfully slow drops of elixir dripped into the bottom. Linnet threw the leech body behind her and tilted the Chalice rim gently to the Queen's ice-rimmed lips. Nothing happened.

'I told you,' snarled the Prince. 'If she dies . . . I will hunt you down forever. I can do that, you know. And I will. Too many of my people have died for you today, Maiden.' Linnet felt as if everything was in slow motion.

Was she herself really going to die after all this effort, hunted by the Prince and his hounds – running for her life for as long as he chose? There were no Maiden memories to help her here – no Maiden had ever been in this situation before. No one had. She closed her eyes. *Think!* she told herself. And then she took her technowatch off and laid it on the Fey Queen's breast, spellwords coming to her as she did so.

'*Tilleadh, o Banrigh!*

Return, O Queen!' she whispered, no certainty in her heart, but only hope and desperation. The spellwords drifted for a long second, and then the watch flared and leapt back into Linnet's surprised hands as if flung, and the ice crystal flowers burst into a riot of bloom. As Linnet put the watch on yet again, very slowly, from the midst of the blossoms rose the Fey Queen, magically restored to her full beauty. The Fey Prince ran to her with a cry and clasped her in his arms, insubstantial as they were.

'So long it has been, *ah!* so long . . .' and he knelt at her feet, along with all the other Fey, who had, it seemed, been restored too by Linnet's spell. The Fey Queen looked at Linnet disdainfully.

'Open the Door, mortal,' she said, her voice as icy as the flower crystals that had so recently covered her. Linnet looked her in the eye for just long enough to make the Queen duck her head in a grudging acknowledgement, and then she did so, making sure that none of her technomagic lurked in wait for the Fey on the other side. Bitter words about ingratitude hovered on her lips, but a new sort of wisdom inside her told her that they would do no good. It was better to let the Fey go back to Avvallon, back to their feasting at Caer Criostal, and their hunt of the White Hart who was really Cernunnos. A thought struck her as a waft of summer flowerscent drifted from the open Door, through which the Fey were now streaming, turning green and solid as they reached the other side. What would they do with Fidget Reedglitter's iceblock? She didn't know. And she didn't really care at this point. If they wanted her to move it, they'd have to ask. But Fidget was definitely never coming back – Linnet's spell would see to that. The Queen would have to find another sorceress to do her royal bidding. Then the last Fey was through, and as he disappeared, the Door snapped shut, leaving the biggest Owlstone as it had always been – plain rock, unadorned with any trace of the way into Avvallon.

Linnet sank to the earth beside it and dropped her head into her hands, leaning against the solidity of stone. It felt real and reassuring – as if it anchored her properly to the earth of her own world for the first time since she had left. Then she started as a soft, feathery something brushed her cheek. Mathafurd looked down at her from Gladysant's back, and bowed to her, his bearded face serious.

'Gladysant and I must go back and report to Caebrolla,' he said. And then he had said some things which made Linnet feel rather squirmy inside – about bravery and gratitude and all sorts of other stuff which eventually forced her to tell him to shut up or else she'd put a silencing hex on him!

Mathafurd just grinned, and threatened to make a song about her instead, and sing it at every possible opportunity. 'I am a bard, after all,' he teased her as she reached up and hugged him goodbye. Linnet just hoped Petroc would never hear him sing it – because that would be really, really embarrassing and uncool. Gladysant allowed her to plant a farewell kiss on her beak (although the hound voices had complained a lot about that), and then they had flown away, disappearing behind Cerne Tump in a flash of sunlight. She would miss Mathafurd, Linnet thought, but he had promised to come and visit her often. As she slumped once more against the Owlstone, the Smith moved over to her and put a comforting arm around her shoulders.

'Come on,' he said. 'Fay will get Zafira home. She won't remember a thing. Let's go and get your mum and dad and Petroc. Don't worry,' he said hastily, as he saw the panic starting in her eyes. 'They're quite safe.' Linnet sighed in relief and looked around her properly for the first time. Professor Hullart lay like a log on the grass in the circle. Rhiannon and the Badger were tending him, and what looked like a whole parliament of hootcat owls were flying round, hooting hysterically, which didn't help her impending headache. Then she squeezed Wayland's hand and nodded gratefully, too weary to speak for the time being. Quite suddenly she wanted her parents really badly.

The Smith gestured the spell as he opened another door in the air, and they stepped through into the Gateway between the Worlds. Three figures lay on the grass at the edge of the pool, fast asleep. Linnet breathed in the sudden green energy of the place. She felt it running through her bones, waking up her blood, making her alive as she had never felt alive before. The Power within her knew at once what this place was, and what grew here. Iddrasgyl, she thought, awed. The Tree that never dies. The Protector of the heart of things. Wayland grinned at her.

'Good feeling, eh? Almost as good as defeating a dirty great worldwyrm singlehanded?' Linnet looked at him, straightfaced.

'Nah!' she said. 'Nothing could feel that good!' Then she noticed the small figure on the island, cradled by Iddrasgyl's roots. Surely it couldn't be? She stepped closer. Yes, it was definitely Magret.

'What's she doing here,' she asked Wayland quietly. 'And why?'

'Rhiannon brought her,' he replied. 'Iddrasgyl will hold her body safe in his roots for ever now.' Linnet found tears running down her cheeks, and she wiped them away, scraping her cheek with her technowatch as she did so. She stopped, looking at it. She remembered her thoughts at the Door.

'I could,' she said slowly. 'In this place where the Tree that never dies grows . . . I could reverse time and make her alive again. I could at least give her that.' But Wayland shook his head firmly, taking her by the shoulders and looking deep into her eyes with a seriousness she had never seen in him until now.

'If you run Time backwards now, you will undo everything you have gained. I don't understand how your new magic works yet, but I do know that. Time is not to be meddled with lightly, unless in great need, as you have already done. That was right – bringing Magret back would not be. Let her rest here. It is not the worst place she could be.'

Linnet kicked at the smooth grass. 'Why?' she shouted, the grief and horror of it coming over her for the last time. 'Why? Was it all my fault? What if I'd become the Maiden sooner – not fought against it? Would that have made a difference?'

Wayland held her against him. 'No,' he said. 'No. Things are as they are, and you cannot and could not have changed them. What you have done as Maiden has saved us all. Hold onto that. It is a great thing.'

Then a sleepy voice came from behind them. 'Linnet,' it said. Then louder. 'Linnet!'

'Oh, Dad!' she cried, running into his arms. Merrilin Perry looked up at the Smith over Linnet's head.

'I suppose I shall have to hold off on killing you now, since my daughter seems to be safe,' he said. 'I think I'll feed you a Brew instead. One of my Specials.'

'I'll look forward to it,' said the Smith. 'Horns and all.' And he smiled at his old friend as Nyneve and Petroc woke up too, and flung themselves at Linnet.

The next hours and days had kept Linnet and the Guardians impossibly busy setting everything to rights – all except Cernunnos, who had kept his promise to the Fey Prince and immediately made his way back to Avvallon for the Hunt. As the White Hart, he was being chased all over Avvallon by the Fey Hounds and the Royal Host, having a great time outwitting them, she suspected. Cernunnos would never be caught – she knew that now, having worried at first until the Lady had explained it to her.

'The White Hart is eternal,' she had said. 'He dies and rises again over and over, and this is a mystery older than even I am, which has its roots deep in the old lore of magic. Cernunnos will be safe. And in time he will return to Cerne Tump, and you can visit him and hear all about it.'

As for Wyrmesbury itself, the petrified residents had been soothed and calmed by a powerful six-pronged Forgetting spell, but Linnet herself would never forget the screaming, huddled mass of terrified humanity they had found there. As soon as she and the others had returned from the Gateway between the Worlds, they and the rest of the Guardians had run across the fields to rescue the town. Neighbours, friends, shopkeepers, people she had known all her life had been huddled in the streets, weeping and hysterical and utterly bewildered at the worldwyrm's terrifying appearance. But now they had all gone back to their usual states of being – contented or not, according to their natures. Whether strange things would still happen in the town now that the worldwyrm had gone, none of the Guardians knew. But Linnet suspected that they might, although maybe in a new way. A place that had held magic for so long would not lose it overnight.

Petroc had not been subjected to the Forgetting magic, and neither had her parents. The older Guardians had decided that she needed at least one person of her own age who understood what she had done and what she was, and Petroc had agreed, although he and she hadn't spent much time together since everything happened – they'd both been busy with other stuff, she with her Guardian work, and he with looking after Zafira. When they had talked, briefly, he'd explained that he didn't want to leave Zafira alone until he was sure she was recovered from her time in Avvallon – even though she didn't remember anything about it. And he'd also looked at Linnet in a funny, considering sort of way – a different way that she had been too preoccupied with other things to work out yet, or even think about.

As for Linnet's parents, they had made their own choice to remember. And she thought that perhaps there was a chance that she might get on better with her mother now. Certainly Nyneve had been treating her as if she was a precious plant that needed special care since they got home. She could see that that could get old quite quickly. Maybe she'd have to do something to bring her mother back to reality. Like nicking some of Dad's Monster Brew and feeding it to Petroc. She laughed out loud as she sat on her bed, remembering the night before.

Wayland had come to supper, as he usually did on a Wednesday. Her father had kept his promise and slipped some of his latest Special into Wayland's beer, when he wasn't looking. Wayland had immediately sprouted horns, and a tail, and really really long purple whiskers down to his feet, which he had immediately tripped over. That had definitely been fun.

As the painstaking work of being a Guardian went on and on and on, Linnet was not so sure that magic was fun at all, though. Everyone in Wyrmesbury now thought it had been just another bad earthquake, and they had been bewitched not to notice the Guardians' mending activities. Neither the Guardians nor Linnet's magic had been able to put the top back on Witches Tor – that had disappeared into the earth with the worldwyrm, but generally speaking, they continued to shore up foundations and retile roofs and generally put everything that the wyrm had damaged or destroyed back together again. Linnet was tired of Repairing magic. She was fed up with Forgetting magic. In fact she was so bored of any kind of magic that it had even been a relief to go back to school after all and learn Frankish verbs with Mr Snawkins.

Lelicia Sundew and Them held no terrors for her now – she knew she could deal with Them on her own, with neither Petroc nor magic to help her. And she had, on the very first day she walked off the bus. They would not ever be friends, but her newly confident attitude had bred a wary kind of respect in Them, and she didn't think They would ever give her any more trouble. She smiled inwardly. They'd better not. She no longer felt like the weirdo of Wyrmesbury, she thought. But on the other hand she no longer knew quite who the new Linnet was now, either.

She straightened, as she gestured the last brick into place in the wall of the little Primary School she had been mending, and walked away from it all, over the summer fields and up the hill called Maiden's Mount, now so familiar and so her own place that as she set foot on its flowery slopes she started to run until she had reached the very top and was sitting by the still pool at its centre.

She sat there for hours, thinking about her new kind of magic and worrying about what she was going to do with it, and how it was going to affect her life. She hadn't wanted to be any kind of hero – and to most people she wasn't. But who was she?

Not a Guardian – although part of their circle. She was too young to ever feel really comfortable with them anyway – even Wayland. It was like having six other parents – nice, but it made her feel rather hemmed in and watched.

Not an ordinary girl ever again – if she'd ever been really ordinary, what with the visions and all, she thought.

Over and over again she tortured herself by remembering that she was the only person in the whole world who had this new magic, and that there was no one else who could truly help her, when she looked up and saw a figure at the bottom of the hill. It was Petroc. He looked . . . hesitant, she thought. Unsure of himself. And she suddenly realised that she'd missed his presence desperately, and that she wanted to see him more than anything or anybody else. Right now.

'Come on up,' she shouted, waving.

'Am I allowed, Maiden?' he called back, sounding strangely formal. Her heart seemed to stop in her chest. Surely Petroc didn't think . . . ? But maybe she'd better do this properly. Just in case. Then he'd know how she felt about him.

'Petroc Suleymann,' she said, Power filling her voice. 'The Maiden welcomes you here. Always and forever.' Petroc winced slightly.

'Please,' she said. 'Please, 'Roc. I . . . I've missed you a lot. I . . . I need you.' And then it was all right, and his long legs were flying up the hill, and she hugged him and hugged him until he begged for mercy and tickled her to make her let go.

'It's so strange,' she said a few minutes later, as they sat together by the pool, dangling their hot feet in its coolness. 'Everything has gone back to normal again – well as normal as it ever is in Wyrmesbury. It somehow feels like nothing ever happened.'

'But it did – you and I know that, and your mum and dad and the other Guardians, even if no one else in Wyrmesbury does,' he said. 'But we've got to get on with the rest of our lives now, and find a way of dealing with it all. You'll always be the Maiden – and I can tell you, it's taken a bit of getting used to, all that magic stuff you can do. Mending and all that, as well as the other technostuff. Useful, but bizarre. But I've been doing a lot of thinking, and you're also still the Linnet I've known all my life underneath.' He reached out and took her hand rather tentatively. 'Still my best friend and . . . and maybe . . .' He gazed at her with that new, strange look, his dark skin now tinged with red as he spoke. 'Maybe something else too. Later on, obviously. If you wanted. When we're older.' His voice died away.

Linnet sat silent and stunned. Of all the things Petroc could have said, she hadn't expected this. What should she say? Then everything came clear.

'You're right,' she said, looking up at him and holding on tightly to the hand which was now clutching her own in a damp and waiting sort of way. 'I'm Linnet *and* the Maiden, but that doesn't have to mean I'm torn in two.'

At the back of her mind, impinging on her thoughts slightly, she could feel her own sort of magic fizzing away, waiting to be discovered. So what if no one else had it? It was not dull old magic which had run out of steam – it was exciting, new, and it was hers to explore and grow into if she wanted to – hers to take into whatever future she pleased. But as of now she didn't have to do it alone.

And that made all the difference.

The chapter headings in *Hootcat Hill* are taken from the following sources:

Chapter Nine from: '*When you see millions of the mouthless dead*' by Charles Hamilton Sorley (1895–1915)

Chapter Ten from: '*Thomas the Rhymer*' Anonymous 17th Century

Chapter Fourteen from: '*The Mermaid*' by Alfred, Lord Tennyson (1809–1892)

Chapter Fifteen from: '*A Midsummer-Night's Dream*' Act ii, Scene i, by William Shakespeare (1564–1616)

Chapter Eighteen from: '*Lalla Rookh*' part vii, The Fire-worshippers, by Sir Thomas Moore (1779–1852)

Acknowledgements

Hootcat Hill has been a long and sometimes tortuous time in the writing, and it also belongs to the following, without whom it would not have seen the light of day:

Firstly, my dear friend Louis, who sent me to Paradise Pier in delicious Donegal – the perfect place to write my (nearly) final full stop. *Tapadh leat, a ghaoil! Tha gaol agam ort.*

As always, the whole lovely children's team at Orion, especially my editor Jon Appleton, a most patient and long-suffering man.

My agent, Rosemary Sandberg, who enthused mightily despite not being a massive fan of fantasy books, and gave me an immense amount of support and advice.

Frank and Alicia Curran, who lent their cottage to a total stranger, fed me yummy food, and let me write unhindered for the last and most important stretch of the book.

The home team – Andrew and Janet – who made sure the wheels didn't fall off my domestic life . . .

And finally, last, but never least, my dearest children, Archie and Tabitha, my godson Dom, and all their friends who read and commented constructively and enthusiastically on early drafts, as did the-best-mother-in-the-world, despite thinking it would be a chore for her (another converted non-fantasy fan!). On to the next book, guys!

L.C.
Northamptonshire,
September 2007